segments, based on their overall financial capacity, operational sophistication, and the general perception of their brands. A good standing across these parameters was often described in the industry as "clout" and the banks with the largest clout got to pick and choose their market segments and, within those, the best customers.

General Bank did not have as much clout as some of its older, or more sophisticated, contemporaries and, therefore, had strategically settled for the troublesome, though profitable, middle-market, thereby consolidating its operational capabilities and marketing communications around this. The Bank often bragged about its leadership of the middle market and how there was none of the so-called leading banks that could effectively compete with it in this space. It wasn't clear; in any case, if any of the leading banks were trying.

Most of the blue-chip companies had access to international financing and, therefore were extremely snooty and quite tough in their negotiation. The middle market customers on the other hand were often, less sophisticated and at the same time less-eligible for global funding, thereby ensuring that their negotiation scope was limited. The middle market, therefore presented a better margin, but these same qualities ensured that the margins came with the commensurate risks of delinquency. General Bank, however, continued to enjoy its mastery of the middle-market along with a pocket of other similarly positioned banks. What these other banks didn't realise, was that the owners and management of General Bank aspired beyond this, and that undercurrent of unrestrained ambition ensured that it ran a particular kind of operation.

Being that oil was the mainstay of the economy, the oil and gas companies commanded the largest business volumes. However, given their reluctance to bank with General Bank and others in that league, competition among these banks for the much smaller middle-market customers was extremely stiff. With cut-throat competition at such levels, the middle-market banks often employed "sharp-practices" in swaying prospective customers to their side and recognising their willingness to bend the rules, the middle-market customers, often sharp-practitioners themselves, played one bank against the other for the juiciest deals, and whenever necessary, press them to push the regulatory envelope. Often times, these sharp-practices tread the fringes of illegality and, with that being the nature of their operations, these banks attracted and promote a certain kind of banker. This elite crop of bankers was known as the 'high-flyers'.

The high-flyer banker, as Disun was quick to learn, was one that understood the silent code guiding the Bank's business. This code, in a nutshell, was to do absolutely anything that may be necessary to mobilise cheap deposits and, in the same token, attract, retain and maximise profits from the most lucrative clients. The high-flyer was one that understood this silent code, including the instinctive ability to determine deemed critical circumstances in which a discretionary flaunting of the regulatory framework would be warranted. Such high-flying bankers were those who were willing to initiate these contraventions, knowing fully well that such infringements were undertaken at their own risk, since in no real-world situation would the Bank acknowledge authorisation of their acts. This intricate high-wire-balancing was often craftily rebranded as aggressiveness, and many bankers would receive implicit authorization from their superiors, and often, the bank's leadership, to proceed upon their own good judgment, knowing that they stood to gain significantly if the plan went well, but knowing also that should their machinations blow over, they were "'strictly on their own".

The typical high-flyer, therefore, was that banker, usually in the market-facing departments, who understood the unique nature of his responsibilities within this unusual code, and, especially, one that was willing to embrace the underlining risks wholeheartedly. Simply, one that was willing to play the game. The high-flyer could be likened to a secret service operative assigned on clandestine missions behind enemy lines, knowing that if he were caught, he would enjoy no support from his handlers. It took a certain kind of personality to operate in this mode, and it was this exclusive niche of bank employees – executive daredevils working in this highly treacherous mode – that rose rapidly within the ranks. These were the eyes of the banks, Disun always remembered. Given that they were typically very limited in number, were these the few that were enlisted on the fast track towards ascension into the banks' leadership?

It all eventually came together powerfully for Disun in one moment of quiet contemplation as he sat at the counter after work and watched the day's operation wind down. So far, he could only identify a single high-flyer in the entire Broad Street Branch of General Bank. This lone-wolf archetype was none other than Jide Doregos. Disun could now understand why Doregos had that aura about him – why he walked around with a chip on his shoulder; because, if anything, Doregos knew for certain whom he was. Disun now understood why he wanted to be this man. For him, this was something like an Epiphany, and from that moment onward, Disun was to define his career aspirations from this singular perspective. He had to be a high-flyer by all means necessary.

Subsequently, Disun begun to think seriously about his career at General Bank. With keen observation of the Bank's leadership and with several rounds of discourse with Foley, he begun to marshal what seemed like a credible plan towards transitioning from a relative nonentity within the industry to becoming someone to be reckoned with. The sessions with Foley were invaluable and he was pleasantly surprised on one occasion when he stepped into their usual after-business rendezvous at a cosy lair by the corner of Broad Street and Tinubu Square called The City Bar to find Foley sitting at a table with none other than Jide Doregos. That night, the conversation took a peculiar turn, veering off to cars, women and various other vanities that powerful men and their admirers pursued. Finally, at the turn of the hour, the subject came back to banking, and especially General Bank. After several glasses of brandy, Doregos' outbursts were fluid, and unrestrained. Disun couldn't have been happier that he happened in on the duo at such a vantage point.

"You both have great potentials," Doregos said as the night wore on. "You're both gifted in different ways, and, without mincing words, you both have a shot at the leadership of this bank. Hopefully, I have enough experience to say this with some measure of credibility. After all, I have been a banker for two decades and, I have spent the last half at General, essentially at the executive level."

Doregos continued to sip his brandy quietly, while his protégés listened with rapt attention, wary of missing a salient point in a moment of careless distraction. "You both have a good chance. You, however, have to work extra hard. In fact, that's an understatement. You have to work like a dog. Work harder and smarter than each and every one of your contemporaries. Actually, to be realistic, you have to work harder than your bosses; and smarter too. Eventually, you will be recognised and invited into the inner circles. If you're lucky and you get transferred to Head Office where you have visibility; or if your activities even at the branch have direct HQ implications, you improve your chances even more. The challenge, though, is that with visibility comes a higher level of responsibility."

"I hear you, Sir," was all that Disun could say.

"At the Head Office, for instance, you cannot hide. You have to look like the big boys, clean, crisp, sharp suits, shirts and ties all the time. You cannot afford a single bad day, because, guess what, that might be the day that you would need to submit a report directly to the MD. You have to remain at your desk deep into the night after all the ordinary folks have left, because, whether you realise it or not, the MD can see you from his CCTV. This is how the players are separated from the clowns. Call it what you may. In fact, call it playing to the gallery, which indeed is what it is – you still wouldn't have changed the reality."

"You also need to equip yourselves. Foley, I know you've been to some of the best Ivy League schools. But you, on the other hand, Disun – you have a lot more to prove. You are bursting at the seams with raw potentials. I can see that. Every time I look at you, I see a performer; a potential high-flyer. But raw potentials and good work can only get you so far. To escape from the prison behind the counter, you have to ramp up you qualifications. You need to get some cardboard. Write some exams. Obtain some degrees. I don't care how you do this and I don't care to listen to your whining about your work, time constraints or any of that lame stuff. Just decide, focus and get it done. A lot of successful bankers did it this way: evening classes; weekends; personal coaches; crash programs. I don't care what you have to do; just do it! Get yourself a degree at the minimum, and then follow up with executive courses. This is an absolute minimum for you; otherwise, you will be stuck at the counter with the ordinary folks. You will be stuck there for life!"

Disun felt Goosebumps as he listened to Doregos. But Doregos called him a potential high-flyer. That was the key – Doregos used the magic words to describe his potentials. That was the key.

The following month, he enrolled at the University of Lagos for an Executive bachelors degree in Banking and Finance. The good news, however, was that the university offered an alternative program running three evenings during the week and full days over the weekend. He couldn't have asked for anything more. It became a dog's world from then on, but with the seed that Doregos had sowed in him that evening, he wholeheartedly embraced the life.

CHAPTER 18

IT WAS A RAINY OCTOBER MORNING as Disun made his way briskly towards his Office. He held his umbrella with one hand and clutched his folder against his chest with the other, struggling to hold his jacket in place while, at the same time, protecting his clothing from the wet wind. He was grateful when No 72A came to sight, and, indeed, near ecstatic when he finally ducked in through its main doors.

By the end of the week, it would have been five years since he commenced his career at the Bank and four years since he enrolled at the University of Lagos. The banking grind had been intense, and his routine for obtaining a part-time degree in Banking and Finance, if anything, had even been much more demanding. At the beginning, it all seemed like an eternal roller-coaster ride, full of endless hours of gruelling class work, back-to-back assignments and nerve-racking term papers. But somehow, he had stuck to it, and somehow, he had prevailed.

Progress had been steady at the office also, with a series of client and supervisor feedback leading to recognition and, finally, rapid promotion. In the midst of all this, Disun continued to solidify his relationship with a crop of high net-worth customers, who, with their loyalty, rewarded him for his commitment to anticipating their needs and serving them relentlessly.

Disun continued to build on his relationship with key customers, helping them with their credit applications, often barging into credit committee meetings at high risk to elicit reasons for delays in the customers' credit application approvals. While those brazen episodes enhanced his courage and gravitas, they also provided unique learning opportunities, since the Senior Executives, encouraged by his confidence, would often sit him down and, show him the causes of the delay, then seize the opportunity to provide context, and lecture him on banking technicalities, guidelines and intuition. By the time the customers showed up at the bank to follow up on their applications, Disun would either have an approval waiting for them, or clear guidance around what they needed to provide to enhance their chances.

"What would I do without you," Chinedu – one of his big-trader customers – would often say. "Honestly, Disun, where would *we* be without you?"

Disun was taking the most advantage of his growing relevance and influence within the Bank, and, especially with the Banks customers. At the same time, his relationship with Foley blossomed, and even more so his association with Doregos. Over the months, Doregos had come to take an extra-ordinary linking to him, and the more Disun's influence within the bank grew and the more he built strong relationships with major bank customers, the more his friendship with Doregos grew. Doregos suggested that Disun's future was not in cash or operations, but rather in Corporate Banking. Within that month, Doregos had facilitated his transfer to the Corporate Banking Department, where, more out of design, rather than coincidence, Disun was posted to work directly under his mentor's supervision. Working directly with Doregos was to further open Disun's eyes into the workings of the Bank, and, crucially, the industry at large.

"You have a bright future, Disun," Doregos once said to him on their way to a client's meeting, sitting at the back of his leathered, air-conditioned, Mercedes Benz. "You have the basic prerequisites to succeed. But you've got to want success at a certain level to move things up a notch. You've got to want to up the ante."

Disun listened attentively.

"Let's start with your appearance, for instance. You are a decent-looking chap. Smart, presentable. But you have to clean up a little bit and acquire that suave, winning appearance of a champion. You need to observe the people who run this enterprise and say to yourself: yeah, I want to look like these guys! Or, better still, you want to *be* like these guys. You need to situate yourself in their world and begin to role-play.

You need to identify the few individuals controlling the Bank and start thinking and acting like them. In reality, you cannot actually be like them at this stage, but that was never the objective. The goal is to imitate them enough to draw their attention. Imitation – they say – is the best flattery. Your goal is to be noticed, and to be seen to show that you get it, and, perhaps, more importantly, that you want it. Your bosses would wear their two thousand dollar Armani suits, naturally, and their thousand dollars Gucci shoes. Clearly, you cannot match these, except you begin to dip your hands into your customers' accounts, which, clearly, again, is a career-limiting plan. Well, at least, not for now." Doregos pulled an amorphous, grin. "These guys spend millions on their power dressing; and rightly so, because they can afford to do so; but also because they have earned the exclusive prerogative to do so. You on the other hand haven't. As such, no one has such an expectation of you. At the minimum, what is expected of you is a pursuance of something that resembled the reality. A spirited quest; something that looked like the real deal. All you want is to send a signal to the leadership of the Bank that you acknowledge them; that you admire them; and that you want to be like them. You then wait on the wings for an invitation; and, if you are lucky to get one, you work your butt off to demonstrate that you're worthy. Luckily for you, you've got someone like myself volunteering to guide you through."

"Thank you very much, Sir."

"You can only thank me with your performance. You have got to prove your worth. You have to demonstrate to me that I am backing the right horse. You need to prove that I am making the right investment."

"I won't let you down, Sir."

"Well, let me be the judge of that. My intuition tells me that you are a winner, a champion; but time, at the end, is the best judge of character."

They arrived at the client's office, and their conversation went into recess. When they returned to the office later that evening Doregos called Disun into his office, asked him to shut the door, took a long hard look at him and said:

"As I said to you earlier, Disun, you are a promising young chap; you really have potential. I want to give you an opportunity. As I have said, I want to bring you fully under my wings." He paused reflectively, then, reached into his drawer with purpose. He came up with a thick wad of crisp Naira notes that he tossed on the desk before him.

"Here. Take time out this weekend and buy yourself some nice business clothes – suites, shirts and all. You need to start dressing like a champion. You are now on the Doregos team. Welcome to the club."

Disun was stunned. He remained silent for several seconds, then, after a stutter or two, found his voice.

"Thank you, Sir. I certainly wont let you down."

"Well, let me be the judge of that."

The following evening after work, Disun brought the episode up with his friend.

"I was just slightly taken aback."

Disun was slouched back on his seat at their favourite bar. Foley was sitting right across the table from him, elbows on the worn wood, fingers clasped in a makeshift bridge upon which his chin gingerly sat.

"I can understand why you might feel a little bit unsettled. A little pressured," Foley said. "But, hey, it is an opportunity, no matter how you look at it. You just have to decide for yourself what you want to do with it. You have to determine how far you want to play the big boys' game. The reality is that, this is all the opportunity that you have to evaluate your position and take a stance. Once you plunge in, there is no turning back. From that point onwards, it's a whirlwind, you're either going to survive and thrive, or you are going to die. It all depends on how much of a player that you can quickly become, and how much of Lady Luck is on your side."

"You are scaring me now, Foley."

"That's not my aim. But these, nonetheless, are the facts. You see, people like Doregos have a role. Do not be deceived by his charm and elegance; and you are doomed if you get carried away by his gentle mien. You do not rise to such an influential position at General, or at any bank for that matter, simply by flashing your charm. To have gone that far, you need to have some hard-core qualities. Incidentally, I know Doregos quite a bit, and I happen to have some insight into his background, and, especially, how his mind works. You see, Doregos has seen your potentials – he's obviously been studying you for a while – and he's decided how he wants to deploy you. It's nothing personal. He needs to sustain his productivity within the bank, and he needs people to achieve this. What they call *good* people. Clearly, you have been hand-picked to be on his network of high-flyers."

"This whole proposition as you have described it, sounds intriguing. Some faculty in my mind however tells me that there is a whole lot more to it. Let me lay this down starkly, Foley. What would Doregos and the rest of the leadership of the bank want from someone like me in return for giving me this opportunity?"

"Well, I am sure he has already alluded to that." Foley paused. He seemed pensive, faraway, as he traced vague, abstract patterns on the frosty wall of his Coca-Cola bottle.

"Well, he sort of put in a hint here and there; nothing concrete; just a lot of abstract stuff. He just kept saying that I would need to prove my worth. I am a bit at loss as to what exactly 'proving my worth' entails."

"Well, I guess you'll figure that out over time. But, truly, Disun, your concerns may not be completely out of place. Then again, really, at the end, all they would require of you is performance. The real challenge is that the yardstick for performance varies from person to person and from circumstances to circumstances and it is often at the assessor's discretion. Don't get me wrong, these performance yardsticks have little or no bearing on the Bank's official performance evaluation process. This is a parallel, system, applied by the leadership of the bank to a chosen few; or, rather, *the* chosen few. It is an extremely high-risk system, but once you accept their invitation – perhaps, just in the way that Doregos has extended one to you – you would be assumed to have voluntarily submitted yourself to this parallel scheme."

"If anything, I think you've just succeeded at confusing me even further."

"I don't have all the answers, Disun, but I have a bit of insight, which I am, obviously, trying to share with you as honestly as I can."

"Well, without prejudice to your intentions, Foley, thus far, you have only been able to bewilder me – and that's putting it mildly."

"I apologise if that seems to be the case, my brother. I'll make another attempt at simplifying this. Bottom line: the Bank is all about making profits. Even then, over and beyond this, the bank is about making quick and easy profits. General Bank – just like other banks in the industry – say all the right things about supporting small businesses and betting on genuine enterprise, and all that fancy corporate-lingo. Yeah, that's what they all say all day long. But, at the end, the chief objective of these banks is to make the highest possible profits at the lowest possible cost and within the shortest possible time. Period. If you have this at the back of your mind, then you have solved half of the riddle. With that in the background, it should logically follow, therefore, that anything that enhances the Bank's ability to operate in this manner is deemed as 'performance'".

"Clearly." Disun nodded as he took an anxious sip from his Coke.

"Secondly, as you know, the Bank's merchandize is money. In the final analysis, the bank is in the business of buying and selling money; buying at a certain rate and selling at a higher rate. Therefore, what the so-called high-flyers perpetually aim to do is to see how and where they could best position themselves within this rather simple value chain, based on whatever they consider to be their individual competitive or comparative advantage. Some aim to mobilise huge, low-cost government and institutional deposits; others introduce interest-enthused merchants of so-called large-ticket transactions to the bank, and help the bank to record extensive profits, much of which is often merely "paper" profits, often going bad down the line. The Bank nonetheless looks good in the interim and, even still, the executives in charge look and *feel* temporarily successful. Before the credit facilities implode and the true nature of the transactions are revealed, the executives would have jumped on the nearest and fastest bus to the next bank, often to a higher position and with a large, vibrant and effervescent portfolio of interest-loving customers, aimed primarily to wow the ordinary execs at the new bank or better still, their clued-in, in-house accomplices, who – in their infinite wisdom – had thought it necessary to hire them in the first place, rather often exclusively for this very reason. So, to answer your question, the ultimate aim is to boost profitability and demonstrate some *mojo* in the industry, no matter how dangerously or how temporarily. After all, everyone else was playing this same volatile, precarious game.

"These two categories of high-flyers are dominated by a crop of employees identified and selected for their so-called positioning, just to execute this kind of work. These, as they are usually called, are *people with pedigree*. I know this for sure because I had once been selected; and, subsequently, I had been saddled with the responsibility of seeking out other candidates from amongst my peers. This was in the earlier days of my career when people like Doregos thought I had the instinct and inclination to be one of their recruits. They specifically seek out new employees with the right background, and groom them up to a pre-defined standard. They are looking for people from a certain kind of family; they want to know where you live; which expensive schools that you went to; whom your father is. They have people who would scour through resumes for known last names. They put a certain premium on the Ivy-league degree, not necessarily because of the quality of the education – which was not in question – but more for the benefit of what it says about the holder's social status. They are interested in the sons and daughters of governors, ministers, members of the Senate, top CEOs, business moguls and the like and they would recruit this kind of people, even when they are the least qualified. Basically, what they are counting on is the business that these young recruits could either generate directly or facilitate through their connections. This is performance, based on the set criteria. These elite kids are the performers."

"Really? Where does that leave someone like me—"

"Hmnn, hmnnn, hmmm!" Foley raised an interruptive finger. "I haven't finished yet. There is another category, and, if I am going to be honest, I think this is where you fit in. This is where they need you. It is another group, entirely. Another shot at performance. Another deal. It is something like a back door into the elite group."

"I see? Tell me about this backdoor group."

"You don't have to be cynical about this, Disun. And trust me, had it been someone else involved, I wouldn't even go there. I however know that you have the smarts to assimilate and understand what I am saying; and you have to take this with a positive mind. This only serves as constructive information to put in your repository and apply as and when due. The less sentimental you are about this kind of stuff, the more you will be able to apply it in the strategic and tactical decisions that you will be making in your career at the Bank, and, conversely, the higher your chances of success. You are my buddy, Disun, and there is no competition between us. So I will be proceeding along this line of conversation only on the mutual understanding that your best interest is thus being served."

"Certainly, Foley. Get on with it."

"Without mincing words, Disun, you fall into the *other* category. And by saying this, I mean, that you are a potential high-flyer, but of a different kind. This other kind is occupied by the so-called presentable, so-called dynamic, so-called resilient, so-called go-getters type of candidate. The Bank also recognises potential performers among an alternative group meeting these set criteria. Therefore, within the General Bank parlance, being presentable would mean, for instance, that a candidate is good-looking, well built or physically endowed in a charismatic way, so to speak. Dynamism would refer, for instance, to an innate ability to adapt in various circumstances – deal with crass traders and speak their language if need be and within the same hour, attend a high-level meeting with the expatriate executives of a major conglomerate. Dynamism could connote a measure of street wisdom. It could also describe the ability or willingness to thread delicately on the thin line of legitimacy. Resilience simply refers to stamina: the ability to literally work like a dog and take all the crap that gets thrown down the ladder. And, perhaps, the most important criteria of all to the Bank: ambition. This is what they insinuate whenever they call someone a go-getter. Ambition is the fuel that binds all these other attributes together and, therefore, makes it possible for this candidate from a very ordinary background, as was often the case, by design rather than coincidence, to rise to a level within the eyes of the Bank where he could now be considered for a place amongst the elite, knowing that he could always be trained and persuaded into doing their bidding – often the worst of their biddings, actually – in such a way that his contribution ultimately equals that of the *bona-fide*. At the end, based on this much stiffer criteria, the playing ground is forcibly and artificially levelled."

Disun listens with rapt attention. He probably wouldn't have noticed if a cobra had crawled into his pants.

"I however said something at the beginning, that is subtle, yet, very, very profound. I would nonetheless understand if you hadn't taken notice. When I introduced this group, I called them potential high-fliers. The emphasis here is on the word *potential,* because unlike it is with the *bona-fide* where the high-flying status is assigned purely on the basis of pedigree, basically automatically; this other group is defined initially on potential, and even when a candidate meets all the set criteria at inception, the high-flyer status would ultimately have to be earned. This, therefore, is where all those attributes come into play, and the more ambitious a candidate is, the quicker he earns his recognition, and, the longer he sustains this ambition, the higher he would rise along the organisational rungs. There is, however, a very thin line between ambition and greed and the higher you climb on this hierarchy, the harder it becomes to recognise this line."

"Frankly, Foley, these theories of yours sound very logical; actually, very plausible. Yet, at the same time, I cannot help but hear it play out like fiction in my ears. While it all sounds so believable, how much of these things actually transpire in reality?"

"One-hundred percent. Everything and more. If you like, you may want to corroborate my theories − as you call them − with any experienced, significant someone within the industry. The question is: how many of these people would be willing to volunteer the truth? See, friend, you are bright enough to understand that I have nothing to gains by misleading you; I have no vested interests, other than what my conscience is pushing me to say to you right now. I have a better appreciation of this industry, simply by virtue of my years of experience and interactions with my dad and people like Doregos. I have only voluntarily exempted myself from the game. Not because it is necessarily a bad game, if you know what I mean, but mostly because I had made a philosophical decision a few years ago as to what sort of life I would like to live and this had allowed me to set my priorities right. You would be correct to say that my background gives me the privilege of choice, but then, when I was confronted with the stark reality of what the high-flying game could truly entail, I knew within the innermost depths of my consciousness that I wasn't cut out for that game. Should I have been born in a more enlightened world, I would rather have pursued a career in the arts; or, perhaps, etched a livelihood out of raising thoroughbred horses. Our society provides very few legitimate options. I mean, you would already know that for a fact. If I complain so deeply – in spite of the opportunities inherent within the family background that I am so fortunate to have – what then might an ordinary fellow say? What other career paths are out there and how many realistic entrepreneurial scenarios are presented? This chronic failure of our society in persistently generating legitimate and sustainable platforms for creating value-adding prosperity has ensured that ambitious young people gravitate only in a few narrow directions. The opportunities for ordinary folk are substantially finite, and the people at the helm of affairs at this bank, and indeed all the other banks, are aware of this. That is what they leverage on. You think they got into those positions by being stupid or fair? They know exactly what it is that they are doing. And that is why a role has been defined for the other type. They understand that this class of so-called performer – encouraged by ambition or greed, depending on your definition of choice – exist. They also know that these kids would do anything to succeed. With a dearth of viable alternatives and with the absence of a strong pedigree to leverage on, the banks provide a rare – ostensibly legitimate – platform for growth and achievement. In return, they literally own these people and, with constant promises of greater profits, promotions and power, they fan the flames of their captives' wanton greed."

Disun nodded in silence; deep in reflection. He could definitely relate to this.

"Wow. This is a whole lot to take in on one night, Foley. You certainly know a lot. Too much, probably."

"Well, it is. And it is what it is. You may be right, actually. I probably know too much already; yet, I have opted out, which creates a rather unique, perhaps awkward dynamic within the Bank. Yet, they cannot just ease me out, because they know who I am; where I am coming from. I am not easily dispensable. I can create a lot of trouble for them. The only thing they can do is to frustrate me out. Which is what I suppose they have been trying to do for the past few years. No promotion; little or no recognition; things like that. I get it, though, and it can be very frustrating. I am already designing my exit plan. But knowing what I know, I feel obliged to share my knowledge with you; share my deepest thoughts, so that you could at least learn a thing or two and know how to navigate your way through this minefield. It is a minefield, my friend. Indeed, it is a maze, built on a minefield. But you can survive, and if you are determined; and, with the right map, you may navigate and your way through. But you cannot engage the game in a mediocre fashion. You are either in wholeheartedly, or you are out. You have to consider your options and make up your mind. When Doregos and his people talk to you about performance, you already know what exactly it is they are expecting of you. You have to think very hard about these things. You have to decide."

"Hmnnn." Disun's head resembled a faulty piston as he nodded occasionally in silence.

"That's it, Disun. Now you know exactly what you are getting yourself into."

"I get you."

"Extraordinary wealth and morality hardly mix. So, the question is not about what is right or wrong. The question is about what you want from life; and you above anyone else is the best judge of that."

"Thanks. I really appreciate this."

Disun spent the following weeks contemplating his life choices with Foley's speech always at the back of his mind. He needn't any complex reasoning to define the crux of his friend's epistle, which, fundamentally, was the need for him to make a firm decision as to where he stood with regards to the banking game. This was easier said than done, given that he was now in full cognisance of what the game entailed. At the same time, the prospect of a routine career at the Bank and the ordinary life that came with it was revolting. It didn't take him long to decide. Whenever the doubts crept in and he faltered, the combined image of his brother spread-eagle in the Makoko swamps in an epileptic fit and the quiet sobbing of his mother as she crouched in a corner, hiding from a ravaging Sebastian was enough to rein him back on course.

CHAPTER 19

IN THE MONTHS THAT FOLLOWED, the Nigerian banking industry underwent a transformation unlike anything that had been witnessed since the evolution of the industry, commencing from the days of the colonial banks, pre-independence. Inspired by a liberalisation of the industry, based on the introduction of Universal Banking Licenses to new and existing operators, banks were encouraged to take on the full spectrum of banking services under the umbrella of a single bank. Prior to this new wave of transformation, the industry had endured a decade of a different kind of change informed by quantum leaps in technological advancement occasioning great strides in the quality of service and massive efficiency gains. Most banks went from operating isolated branches across the country within operationally segmented structures where these branches functioned as mini-corporations of some sort and ran fairly independent operations. In that scenario, Branch Managers were lords unto themselves and they ruled supreme on the business and clientele of their branches. In those dark days of banking, a visit to the bank simply for a small cash withdrawal could warrant great preparation and planning, and upon arrival, a hapless customer would be issued with a tally number after which he would be ushered into a pride of place within an endless queue of fellow customers, who would linger on to chat, snooze, wake, and essentially carry on with their entire routine for the day, languishing in the snail-paced queue while a rusty old banking operations officer routinely made his way into the back-office archives and buries himself in a mountain of creased, mouldy files and log-books, tracking, processing and recoding their respective transactions. Perpetually frustrated, customers were know to jokingly urge one another to bring their sleeping mats along the next time they were coming over to the bank for the next transaction, and when the banking halls eventually get steamy with heat and tension and the customers run out of humour, massive fights would erupt. These fights would enhance the Branch Manager's perverse sense of majesty and he would come out from his chamber, rolling his pot belly, pacifying the fighters and promising, like a saviour, that everything would soon be alright. This chaos was sustained until technological progress ushered in the "on-line-real-time" phenomenon, and all of a sudden, the banks' back-office operations were automated, drastically compressed and collapsed into a central location at the Head Offices. Without warning, the back-office monstrosities disappeared, and, inherently, the size and scope of Branch Operations. Along with this new trend, branch staffing was drastically cut down and after great resistance and failed attempts at justification, Branch Managers had little choice but to cede their long-abused powers. With improved services becoming commonplace and redundancy rearing its head at every chance, competition amongst and within the banks reached unprecedented levels, such that work hours gradually crept up and along went the workload of every bank employee. For those who withstood the wave of rationalisation and widespread purges that swept across the industry, survival became a day-to-day preoccupation, and for those who had neither the pedigree nor the patronage of a staunch godfather either within the industry, within the clientele or in government, the imperative to survive was even higher. The industry thus evolved a dog-eat-dog culture, and, when push came to shove, bankers were willing to do whatever was necessary to keep their jobs. More often than not, the definition of necessity was the exclusive prerogative of the few people at the top.

Thus went the first wave of changes in the banking sector to which Disun was a live witness, and, a survivor. What he may have lacked in privilege, he over-compensated for in resilience, and with the psychological skewing and stamina that came with day-to-day life in the neighbourhood, surviving came naturally. After five years of playing this high-wire poker game, Disun emerged on the other side, sore, scarred, surly, but, by then, an avid master of the intricate quasi-political contest that, by then, had become the hallmark of survival in the industry. He however wouldn't have gone that far without the support and encouragement that he constantly received from Doregos.

Coming from the trying years of automation and rationalisation, this new wave of transformation in the sector was less unsettling. If the first wave of changes could be described as an arduous marathon, the current changes could be seen as a leisurely trot. At this point, Doregos had brought his wings and he was in for the ride. Not only had their relationship blossomed at the professional level, they had also developed the semblance of a proper friendship despite their organisational hierarchy. With all the leading banks scrambling for Universal licences, the banking industry was engulfed in a fresh wind of energy fuelled by competition and greed. This competition manifested in a gust of recruitment wars, with the banks trying to out-do one-another in attracting the best talent to drive their revamped strategies and cueing in on this opportunity, banking professionals took full advantage.

One warm Monday morning, Disun walked into the office, settled at his desk and found a yellow post-it note on his computer screen screaming "SEE ME!" It was initialled by Doregos. He went straight into Doregos' office and met the latter slouched on his plush leather seat, feet crossed on his desk TV remote control flicking in his hand as he flipped through the news channels. This wasn't Doregos' typical style. He wasn't one to be actively watching CNN on a Monday morning. Doregos was one to be hunkered down at his desk, trying to substantiate the manifestly expensive lifestyle that he had perpetuated over yet another weekend, by, essentially, justifying his role within the bank. Something had to be very wrong!

"Sit down." Doregos said, his voice soft, his attention still affixed to the TV.

"Trust all is okay, Sir?" Disun's eyes were anxious as he took a seat across the desk from his boss.

"All is well, Disun," Doregos said, lining the remote control perfectly next to the carefully arranged row of cellular phones on his desk. "In fact, all just got better."

" I hope so, Sir." Disun said. "You seem unusually relaxed for a Monday morning. Knowing you well, Sir, you would have been neck deep in work by now."

"Well, trust me, I am neck deep in work at all times. Work doesn't always translate into a flurry of activities...empty scribbling and hand movements. False bellowing of instructions, all that BS. You know how it is. That is necessary sometime, but at some other times, the most effective kind of work is mental. Calm, quiet, intellectual work. The best work is done quietly, Disun. I hope you will always remember that."

"Certainly, Sir…"

"I trust you would. And, that is precisely why I asked you to see me. Because even though work goes on and will continue to go on, it would cease to continue within the four walls of General." Doregos looked away from Disun for a moment and fixed his gaze on the small portrait of his wife and two sons on the console beside him. Disun could picture him – probably – contemplating images of his many silent mistresses in his eyes mind, surrounding that of his family in an aberrant cyst.

"Aren't they beautiful?" He said, seeming to drift away with his family for a while.

"They are, Sir," Disun ventured. He had his suspicions concerning the direction in which Dorego's prologue was leading, but cautioned himself, lest he should jump into the wrong conclusions. "But I am a bit lost on the import of your last-but-one statement, Sir."

"Which one…?"

"Your comment about ceasing to work within the four walls of General and so on, Sir…"

"You're a sharp guy. Disun. I'm sure you've already figured it out."

"Well, your pronouncements seem clear enough, Sir. I am just struggling with the implications a little. Perhaps because it is coming to me rather as a surprise."

"Don't let anything surprise you, Disun. Ever. Always consider all possible scenarios well before they play out; always be prepared. Always have a response. It is called scenario planning. You must always be one step ahead of all possible events."

"I hear you, Sir."

"So, there it is. I am leaving General for greener pastures. I am leaving to pursue a rare opportunity. The Bank's leadership will not be happy, but this is not the time to be sentimental."

Disun was silent. His mind racing, shuffling between a dozen possible lines of response.

"You don't have to say anything. You don't have to be clever. This is just for your information. I tendered my resignation this morning and I am about to commence exit discussions with the folks up there. Obviously, they would want me to stay, and they will come up with all kinds of enticing propositions. But all of that would be futile. My mind is already made. Quorum Bank made me an offer that I – indeed, I guess no one in his right mind – could refuse. I have already accepted, in any case. There is no turning back now. An Executive Directorship, with a six-digit U.S. Dollars salary, a villa in Ikoyi, a four-man domestic staff, two official cars, first class travel and profit sharing trumps anything that General could ever offer me. Trumps anything that General could ever offer you. Which takes us to the next question…"

Disun could hear his heart thumping in his ears.

"Are you willing to embark on this journey with me?"

There was an extended moment of silence. Disun knew that this was a turning point in his life. His response one way or another had significant implications.

"You do not need to provide me with an answer right away, but if you are willing, I am definitely interested in literally carrying you along. I can easily negotiate a Deputy Manager position for you. That would be two levels above your current level – effectively, a double promotion. You'll have to wait another three to five years to achieve that here. It would be unwise not to consider."

"It definitely looks attractive, Sir."

"I would think so and in addition to the promotion and salary increase, you continue to enjoy my guidance. What more could a young man in your current position ask for?"

"I am certainly intrigued, Sir."

"I would be, if I were you."

Doregos' cellular phone let out a frantic shrill, interrupting their *tête-à-tête*.

"Hello," he said, putting a silencing finger to his lips. After about a minute of indiscernible conversation with the party on the other side, he hung up and got on his feet. "So, I guess that is it. Think about this and let's have another chat tomorrow. I have to see the MD now."

"Okay, Sir."

Doregos left the office hurriedly.

The following month ushered in the beginning of a new career at Quorum Bank with Doregos in the lead, and Disun dutifully in tow. This progression however was not assumed purely out of blind loyalty and a sense of obligation to Doregos, but more out of the sighting of a rare opportunity. As Doregos rightly suggested, ignoring such an opening would have been idiotic. The new role at Quorum – at the Deputy Manager level – came with much higher responsibilities, including frequent marketing and negotiation meetings with high-profile clients, direct reporting requirements to Doregos and other Executive Directors and supervisory responsibilities to at least eighteen subordinates at any given point in time. Disun had never assumed so much responsibility throughout the course of his career and had never been saddled with so much tireless, backbreaking work. But every time he fought exhaustion and needed encouragement just to get through the day or, indeed, the hour, he merely needed to take a glance at his brand new Raymond Weil watch to check how much more time he had to file in his next deliverable; or pick up his Motorola cellular phone to call for some snacks from one of the adjoining fast-food bars; or, better still take a long-nagging break, slip into his Calvin Klein jacket and grab the key to his brand-new Honda Accord for a drive to the *Suya* spot further along Broad Street. These perks and privileges made it all worthwhile, and Disun was fast cultivating a taste for the little material things of life. Progress came with its baggage – Doregos was fond of saying – but the many privileges helps to put everything into perspectives. Thus far, Disun had found no reason to dissent, nor had he found reason to complain. With a fresh start at Quorum and with a surfeit of ambition flowing through his veins, he surely but steadily began to consolidate his position within the fabric of the Bank's organisation.

"You have to be a formidable force in order to be relevant, Disun."
Doregos would always say. "You cannot simply be a bystander. You are
already looking the part. Definitely a far cry from the rather rustic lad that
I met at General." He indulged himself in a momentary snicker. "And, I
am giving you complements now, because you have come a long way
indeed. But this is only the beginning. You ultimately have to establish
yourself as a force to be reckoned with. And by this I mean someone who
is relevant. To remain relevant, however, you have to get fully into the
politics. Every situation involving people, positions and property is
inherently accompanied by immense power play. Politics. You may
choose to stay out of the politics and remain insignificant; or get involved
and gain recognition. Every industry has its intrigues. Every organisation,
every household, even. Our banking industry and our banks aren't any
different. General had its politics and so does Quorum Bank. The more
you rise, the more important your political game becomes. The more
crucial it becomes. There are the statutory guidelines, as written – Banking
and Other Financial Institutions Laws, they call it – and most banks base
their operations and code of conduct upon this; but there is also the silent
code, accessible to and understood only by the players; those who truly
run the affairs. You cannot succeed exclusively through the strength of
your abilities: technical competence, work ethics or stamina. Those could
only take you so far. To be accepted by the powers-brokers – you have to
demonstrate your capacity as a partaker. In order to even have a legitimate
chance to do this, you have to engage the politics, headlong. And, at some
point, to further prove your worth, you have to be able to do some *Odu*.
This goes side-by-side with the politics. It is even more important in
certain instances."

"What do you mean by *Odu*, Sir?"

Doregos smiled a long, knowing smile. "You will learn as you
proceed, Disun. You cannot take it all in in a single day."

The following month provided a unique learning opportunity, as
Doregos would put it, as he made good on his promise to take Disun with
him on one of his numerous overseas trips, having earlier assisted him in
procuring an international passport.

"You're getting there," he said, with a big, sly smirk on his face as
they left the office at close of business and approached his car. "You're

fast becoming a full package. Certainly, international exposure always helps."

Doregos' driver was in wait, eager to receive their luggage as they settled into the plush leather comforts of the back seat of his car, with Disun making sure to be on the right side of the backseat, behind the driver, studiously avoiding the traditional owner's-corner. This was another in the growing list of trifling etiquettes that he had fast picked up as he mingled more with super executives and better understood the subtle cultural nuances that they held dear.

The ride to the airport to catch their British Airways flight to London was plagued by periodic traffic jams, Dorego's subtle but stern instructions to his driver, were incessant, often inducing panicky errors by the latter, warranting even sterner instructions. The ride was long and strenuous, but time seemed to have simply whizzed by. Despite the silence in the car, Disun's mind was besieged by flashes of his recent life – panoramic visions of his journey from the muddy streets of Makoko to the marble floors of the Broad Street blocks. He had come a long way. Life on the Street was exhilarating. Every once in a while, he agonised about late nights at the office, as well as the daily early morning rise; but waking up on the crisp, freshly-laundered sheets of his bed in his newly furnished flat always helped him to focus, and whenever he stepped into the comforts of his corporate-loan-assisted Honda, the aroma of the synthetic-leather helped him to put things into perspectives. Just the previous week, he had driven back to the neighbourhood in the Honda to show it to his parents and secure their blessings and, in spite of his fairly ordinary objectives, the journey turned out to be yet another revelation.

He had parked the car on the main road and did the half-mile walk through the myriads of corridors and alleys to his parent's compounds, as he would inevitably have had to do, and he had barely shown his mother the car keys before she had broken into an unknown song and an alien dance, resembling something that a mother-hen would do around her newly hatched chicks. Inadvertently, she had summoned the entire population within the compound, which had summarily surrounded her as she spun around continually, singing one triumphant, adversary-taunting ballad after another, and resembling a burly lop-sided *ikoto* as she spun. Finally, she had grabbed her son by the arm and made her way out of the compound towards the road with the crowd closely behind, gathering mass as it went like a burgeoning snowball. By the time they arrived at the car, it had become a fanfare. An effervescent, ogling, new-car-enthused crowd came with its embarrassments, and while Disun strained to separate the credibly pleased from the deceitful, he also somewhat regaled in the prestige of being the centre of attraction. Perhaps, even more than his own self-aggrandisement, he felt deep contentment in the pleasure of witnessing the joy on his mother face, the obvious pride on his father's and the disfiguring scowl on their envious rivals'. The news of Disun's new car spread through the neighbourhood like an avalanche, and as the cheerful crowd made its way back to the compound in celebration, they scampered past Sebastian's house. Though he would never join in with a philandering crowd of any kind – as was customary with him – this time, Sebastian was on his balcony, watching the procession as it went. Disun did not miss the peculiar expression on Sebastian's face – that expression of unconscionable pain, which a thin line of plastic smile did very little, if anything, to conceal. For the rest of his days, he would live to cherish those few odd seconds when he had fixed his gaze smack on that expression and, gallantly, soaked it all in. If coming back to Makoko in a gleaming Honda Accord had brought such pride to his family and such calamity to their enemies, then it was worth every kobo that he had spent acquiring it, and, even more so, every compromise that he had made in earning it.

They arrived at the airport much later than planned, but Disun did not even realise it. With a mind full and vibrant throughout the journey, who could care less about traffic? Up till the point when the sputtering lights of the Muritala Mohammed International Airport's terminal sprung into his line of sight, he had lost all concepts of time and place. He was further awakened by the shrill noise of Doregos' cellular phone and he was relived that the latter was quick to respond.

"Hello. Yes, it's Doregos… Ah, Your Excellency. How are you, Sir? Well, I am just arriving at the airport. I am scheduled to be in London tonight… Really? Wow. That's really a tough call, Sir. I am at the airport as I speak. If I may crave your indulgence, Sir… Is it possible to reschedule this meeting for Tuesday? I am back on Monday … I'm only gone for three days … Wow. Really tough, Sir … but, who am I to say No. Well, we've got to do what we've got to do. Guess I'll have to call my travel agent right away and re-schedule my trip. I will join you at the house in about an hour. Okay then, Sir. Regards." Doregos hung up the phone looking drained and ruffled.

"What's the matter, Sir?"

"There's a change of plan," Doregos said, visibly exasperated. "I have to be at a meeting with the Chairman of Lang Group. His Lebanese partners are in town and he wants us all to meet to discuss the financing of their new plant. The reality is that these guys are only around for a couple of days, and he said he had been trying to reach me all day. Tough. As it were, we only have tonight."

"Wow. That's really tough, Sir. So what are you going to do?"

"Well, there is no alternative. I just have to suspend this trip." Doregos paused for a moment, thinking. "Now, here's the plan: I will call the travel agent now, and schedule a flight for tomorrow. The booking for tonight is already a no-show, but losing a few thousands on a ticket is nothing compared to what we stand to gain from this deal. As it were, you would have to proceed to London ahead of me. You already have the hotel and booking details. You can just pick up a taxi from the airport. I guess I'll leave my luggage with you so I can travel light in the morning. Everything I need is in my hand luggage. I will catch the first flight in tomorrow and we can take it from there. You just go ahead, get some rest and prepare yourself for a very busy few days; now that we are going to be running slightly behind schedule."

"Okay, Sir." Disun felt the full weight on his new predicament press down on him. He was already nervous from the intricacies of his first international travel. The knowledge of having to do it alone was unbearable. But you didn't earn laurels in the industry by showing timidity in such situations. Situations such as these present rare opportunities to shine.

"Here." Doregos said, handing him a wad of currencies. "That's a thousand Pounds. I know you already have some personal travel allowance, but this would further lessen your pain."

Disun smiled a little, already feeling some ease. "It sure would, Sir."

The Mercedes pulled up by the Departure kerb and, as he disembarked, Dorego's driver was quick to discharge the luggage.

"Okay, then. Be a good boy. You would have sufficient opportunity to be a bad boy once we're done with business." Dorego ventured a charming wink. "But you need to remain focused for now."

"I hear you, Sir," Disun's smile had acquired some confidence by now. He was already easing into the independent traveller mode. After a firm handshake with Doregos and a pat on the back, he grabbed the luggage, turned around and headed for the automatic sliding doors at the Terminal.

"London, here I come," he sighed, battling a coalescence of nervous and enthusiastic vibes.

A streak of maize-yellow sunlight cut through a tiny gap in the curtains with laser-sharp precision, creating a kaleidoscopic shimmering across the room as it dispersed, and, inevitably, waking Disun up. The digital radio-clock on his bedside locker blinked 12:17pm. The alarm had gone off at 7:00am and he had barely managed to reach out, eyes still closed, and flicked off the switch, just before rolling over to the other side of the bed. He wriggled around for a few minutes, and – finally, yielding to the nagging allure of "just-a-few-more-minutes" – drifted off, once again, into slumber-land. In no time at all, he was sprawled in the centre of the king-size bed, in a classic De-Vinci pose, unconscious, drooling and delightfully lost; until, four hours along, he had been brusquely awakened by the usurping ray of light once gain.

The flight to London was not any different from the several that he had, by then, taken in the company of Doregos to important meetings in Abuja and Port Harcourt. The similarities, however, only went that far as he was to realise the minute he set his foot in the terminal at Heathrow. Rather to his amazement, he was able to navigate his way through the terminal, through immigration and customs and all the way to the taxi pick-up point with relative ease and without the need to explain his visit as he had anticipated. He knew immediately that he was in a different world. He could really grow into this jet-setting lifestyle.

The half-hour taxi-ride to the Marriot was just as revealing, and though he usually liked to be engaged in conversation by the taxi drivers on all his travels, he was glad that the Pakistani man at the wheels – on this occasion – was as silent as he was. What he needed that morning was a quiet, scholarly appreciation of the wide gap between the world that he left behind in Lagos – barely a few hours earlier – and this new world that he was just about to navigate; hopefully, discover. This wasn't a time to engage in social jabbering and conscious assimilation of the myths and fables that all taxi drivers – especially the ones plying airport routes – were renown to readily volunteer. This was a time for sober reflection. Upon arrival at the hotel, he had sped through check-in and, in no time, was snuggled into the comforts of the fluffy, king-size bed.

Finally, Disun pulled himself out of bed. Rising late had its merits. He felt well rested. He made his way to the gym, and, after taking a quick shower, had brunch and went on a leisurely stroll down the road. It was an hour before he retuned to the room to be met by a message on his answering machine from Doregos:

"Hi. This is Jide Doregos. I am in the Hotel. Room 710.

Please bring my suitcase along.

Thanks."

Disun smiled a deep, warm smile. His fondness of Doregos was growing. He grabbed the suitcase and made for his bosses room.

"Hey Disun. Just look at you!" Doregos burst out from the bedroom, through what seemed like a kitchenette, into the suite's living area. He looked every bit a billionaire in his white Versace shirt and red linen pants. He held a cocktail glass gingerly in one hand and a smouldering cigar in the other. He seemed a completely different man on this other side of the world, but then, by all indications, very comfortable. "Trust you are enjoying your debut into the world of international travel. Actually, your debut into the world! London definitely is a good way to start. Trust me, you just opened a new chapter of your life. You will look back in ten years and thank me from the bottom of your heart."

"I am already thanking you, Sir."

"You haven't even begun to thank me, trust me. This is merely an introduction. The tip of a potentially rewarding iceberg. Have a seat, Disun. Make yourself comfortable."

The two men settled into two of the ample armchairs, and as Doregos set his glass down on the side table and drew deftly at the base of his *Monte-Cristo*, he said. "Now, where's my suitcase?"

"Right here, Sir." Disun said pointing to the case that still sat by the door. Where should I put it, Sir?"

"Bring it right here, beside me."

Doregos scrolled a combination into the plastic case's locks and popped them open. Then, with an air of exuberance, Doregos flipped the lid open and, in one sift swoosh, revealed a pile of dollar bills. There were dozens of wads arranged one on top of the other, in a smooth, clean, symmetrical array. Disun was staggered by the spectacle before him. He sat up at the very edge of his seat.

"Sir, was this what I was carrying all along?"

"Unless I am a magician, then the answer to your question, young man, is a resounding yes."

"All these wads of dollars? These must run into hundreds of thousands."

"To be precise, One Million U.S. Dollars in cash and another half a million in gold and jewellery."

Disun's mind was racing, trying to decide what to make of these revelations. While one part of him was grateful for the privilege of the trip, another part was full of resentment. In that moment, the realisation that he had been used as an unwitting beast of burden in a money-laundering operation had sown a seed of discord in his heart. He felt betrayed, and this growing sense of betrayal was threatening to manifest in an uncontrollable, explosive rage. In a desperate bid to gather his thoughts, he remained silent and watched quietly as Doregos laid out the stack of currency on the coffee table, commencing an elaborate bulk-counting performance. The silence in the room was poignant as Doregos went about his business with the dexterity of a blackjack dealer, hands moving in synchrony, mouth seeping cigar smoke in various directions.

"Say what's on your mind," Doregos ordered out of the blue.

Disun didn't know what to make of his boss's gambit. He bought some thinking time. "I'm not sure what you mean, Sir."

"What's going on in your mind? Perhaps, I already know what you're thinking. I'm just saying that you should say it out loud like a man. That way, you would, at least, feel better, rather than just stewing away in your own bile."

"I don't think that there is any such thing, Sir," Disun's voice had acquired a bit of an edge, "I would, however, have expected to have been carried along if I was to be saddled with a responsibility of such magnitude."

"Really? You needed to be carried along?" Doregos snickered. "Tell me, carried along to what end? So that you can sit down, contemplate and decide?"

"Something along those lines, Sir."

Doregos laughed again, at first, quietly. Then his entire body was seized by what seemed like a demonic fit of laughter, contorting his face into strange forms, rocking him in all directions and bringing a well of tears streaming into his eyes. Disun watched in silence, battling a coalescence of conflicting emotions.

"Really? What do you think this is, a circus?" Doregos paused to re-kindle his cigar. "You actually think you have a choice?"

Disun was smart enough to recognise a rhetorical, booby-trapped line of questioning. He remained silent.

"I am hoping that you didn't think that this was a circus; or, rather, that I am a clown. I am hoping that you aren't one either."

Doregos started to laugh again. Disun didn't know what to make of his theatrics.

"Now what do you think that this whole industry is all about? If nobody has told you already, and if you haven't figured it out yet, then, I hate to burst your bubble. Believe it or not, this entire industry is a farce and you, my friend, are part of the grand scheme."

Okay. Point made, Sir, Disun was thinking to himself. So, what had all that to do with you planting illicit baggage on me and setting me up for a lifetime in a foreign jail? He however remained silent.

"Allow me to educate you a little, Disun." Doregos crossed his legs on the coffee table and puffed leisurely at his cigar. "The Banking Industry, of which you are a bona-fide operative, is not exactly how you see it. Very few of these banks aim to make any substantial profits, really. Very few are driven by genuine commercial principles. At best, the majority are set up to support their billionaire founder-chairman's core businesses – commodity trading, oil-and-gas, a bit of quasi-manufacturing, you know, all those things that we are constantly pretending to finance. At worst, a few of these banks' chief operations are based on borderline illicit goals. Unauthorised trawling, bunkering, Forex-trading, round-tripping, money laundering and, believe it or not, real Pontzi schemes."

Disun stood in a state of shock, not quite believing what he was hearing, the hope of a few moments ago now turning into utter despair. He wanted to tell Doregos to stop, he didn't want to hear any more of the dream shattering, deflating news, but he was too gripped with panic and disappointment to trust his own words.

"Many of these banks are not set up to make profit from their core banking operations, but as they operate in the negative day-in-day-out, they are serving their primary purposes, which is to attract cheap deposits from the unwary public to provide cheap credit to their cartel of owners and their cronies. Do you not read about the perpetual chain of scandals in the newspapers? Could you not read between the lines? All that regulatory hype about single-obligor limits and so on is just a charade. What does it take to have a company register fifteen small subsidiaries and affiliates and spread a billion Naira loan across these entities? Are the regulatory inspectors able to discern? Or better still, are they willing? Ask me, why is it that even when these contraventions are discovered and the culprits caught, isn't the case such that the Managing Director of the erring bank only gets a slap on the hand, or that the chairman gets suspended for a few months, or he is asked to step down only to be replaced by his brother-in-law or his best friend? It is all a sham, my young banker friend. This industry is built on vice. You need to shed this saintly cloak that you have donned, otherwise, you will not survive."

The full import of Dorego's revelations weighed down on Disun's psyche. His conscience was being torn in all directions. As he grappled with the subliminal battle of ethics, he was not lost on the fact that he had only just been drawn him into criminality, albeit unwittingly.

"All this is new to me, Sir. This is baffling stuff."

"Well, you had better listen and learn. Nobody will ever show you what I am currently revealing to you. Nobody will ever take you into their confidence on these kinds of things. What would have happened in reality is that you would have learnt slowly, over the next decade or so, and you would have learnt the hard way. By the time you realise that this game is a charade and that you are the ultimate pawn, it would have been too late. You would have worked yourself to infirmity, made little or no money, have no pensions worthy of that name, and if you are not careful, wind up fired or in jail. But I know your story and I want to help you. It is not my style to say things like this, but I generally like you. I like you simply because I see a lot of me in you. You are, at the moment, where I was many years ago, and what I learnt the painful way, I have chosen to share with you for free. Everybody needs a break in life every once in a while."

Disun wasn't sure whether to be grateful of disdainful. "Well, I thank you Sir."

"Don't thank me yet. Just listen and learn."

"Yes, Sir."

"The whole banking industry is not what it is put out to be. How many times have we given loans to customers when we all knew from the outset that they were in no position to pay back? How many white-elephant projects have we financed? This game is not always about viability, nor is it always about profitability. All of that, my friend, is fallacy. Don't you ever wonder how come everyone reports losses at the end, yet, no bankruptcy is declared; no banks are defunct? Nobody goes to jail; somehow, everybody still wins. The regulatory folks know that the game is on. Do you think that they are stupid? What do they care? Nobody really gives a damn. They themselves are in on the game, if you really want to know. That is the cold truth. Everybody is neck-deep in grime. So long as a bank barely keeps its liquidity ratios; or barely stays just below its single obligor limits; so long as some foreign rating agency had been encouraged to post a mediocre BB rating for the country's credit worthiness; so long as there is a perceived sense of stability within the population; and, so long as there is a balance of some sort induced by an artificial equilibrium – no matter how fragile – the jamboree continues. Everybody smiles home at the end. But how do you think that this fragile equilibrium is maintained? Everybody that's anybody in this economy is clued in. Eventually, when it's time to bust the bubble, the core players are the first in the know. They are the first to exit, clean their positions and tidy up. When the cookie begins to crumble, they are already in the clear. They would have transferred their key interests abroad, or taken solid positions in new, more viable local holdings. What are proxies for? When the bubble bursts, you cannot trace anything to them. And if by any chance you were to find any undoing, it would have been set up to have occurred within the regular course of business. Honest mistakes, they would have been termed. If for whatever reasons, there were some loose ends, or if – for instance – one of the designated fall guys refuses to play ball and spills the beans, then there would only be a legal tussle. These folks know how to hire the best lawyers; hire the best judges, if need be; get important people to make important phone-calls; work the system; organise emergency wee-hour meetings and call old favours. Even if they were to be tried and sentenced, it would all have been a travesty. So, what do you think we are talking about here?"

Once again, Disun was at a loss as to whether this was a rhetorical question or one that was intended to elicit a response. He was rescued by the sudden resumption of Doregos' tirade.

"When push comes to shove, who stays on to clean the mess? Who do you think the fall guys are? Of what mettle do you think fall guys are made? Make no mistake, my ambitious little banking protégé; the fall guys are you and I. We are the fairly anonymous people. People with no big legacy names to be besmirched by a scandal. Low impact guys. We are the sacrificial lambs. However you may be inclined to look at it. Perhaps I am a different kind of fall guy now, but I wasn't born with a silver spoon. My father never had a single share in this bank, nor any bank nor company for that matter. I worked my way up the ladder. I now look like the owners of the bank, dress like them – better than them the vast majority of the time. Now I know a thing or two about the game; even know some tricks that they themselves have no clue about. That's because I am far hungrier than they are; far hungrier than they could ever be. And even though I am now quite comfortable financially, I have consciously remained hungry. I have experienced the indignity of poverty, first hand, and, I am never going back there. Period. It's as simple as that. These guys tolerate me because I deliver, but they are perpetually wary of someone like me. They know where the difference lies. They know that I am made of a completely different material, of a completely different spirit. No matter how they try, they could never be like me; they could never be as ambitious; never as relentless. The truth is that they have never been truly hungry and they don't know how to go back to that mental place; that place of fear, want and deprivation. I, on the other hand, know how to go there. In fact, I am still there, every day of the week as I do these deals. And, they know these things. They are as confident as death, that if the opportunity presents itself, I will take the bank from them."

Doregos got on his feet and disappeared momentarily into the interior of his suite. He returned with an ornate bottle of some strange liquor and replenished his glass.

"So, they have prepared a place for me, as they have for you. Your career has been pre-determined. Your destiny at the bank, pre-set. People like you are preordained for a particular role. You are the guy that would become the go-to guy, high-flying, risk-loving guy; the clean-up guy and for as long as you continue to be useful, to be relevant, you will enjoy the perks and privileges that come with this role."

Disun sat still, contemplating this strange and frightening revelations that were unfolding before his eyes.

"When the going is good, you are the guy that constantly stays ahead of the game," Doregos continued, "you are the guy that stays awake after the other folks have tucked themselves deep under their duvets rollicking with their wives and concubines. It is you, wise man! It is you and I! *It is we!* We are the ones that have to keep our big, red bulgy eyes peeled. Brains ticking, jugular pulsating all night long, threatening to wake up the wife or the entire neighbourhood. However, you are also the dispensable guy. When you have outlived your relevance, you are the easily disposable guy; you are the fall guy. You and I? Or hasn't your sharp go-getting brains figured that out yet? Okay, perhaps I should rephrase that a little. It is I, and, to a lesser extent, you, for now. But it would soon be your turn."

There was a long moment of silence while Doregos re-filled his glass and paced the room evocatively. Then after a few sips at his cocktail, he resumed his tirade.

"The aim of this long speech, Disun, is to begin to prepare you for the inevitable; the clear future ahead of you. These are the things that are yet to come, but that would, without any iota of doubt in my mind. The absolute bottom-line is that it is people like us who do the heavy lifting; it is we who do the hard and dirty work in the bank. It is people like us who are required to engage in the tricky deals while, at the same time, making sure that all the bases are covered. It is I who constantly stay ahead of everyone; make sure that all interests are upheld. It is I who keep the equilibrium. And how do you think I get compensated for all these acrobatics? How do I get to maintain this wonderful, jet-setting lifestyle? You think I leave on my great banking salary? Don't be stupid, young man, and frankly, I know you aren't. I assume that you already get the gist of my sermon. It is however still important that we are on the same page, so that you do not build your career on a false pretence and mess things up for yourself and for everyone. Which is the point of this trip and this entire half-hour rant on my side. This is what this game is all about. You do not get to the top just by being a nerd or working yourself silly. You have got to be worthy. You have to be one that could be trusted."

Doregos dragged the suitcase to the middle of the sitting area. "That takes us back to this elegant suitcase that stirred the conversation. This is what we have to do, Disun. This is our role. This is our destiny. This here is an example of how we gain recognition and, believe it or not, respect. And this is how we take advantage of the system, and create a fallback position, just in case things go awry, which it often does. You can call it what you like, but the point is that we ultimately have to play both sides. For as long as there are people bent on taking money out of the country and those bent on bringing money in, there will be people like us. This is just one of the several tools at our disposal to gain relevance and profit from our indignity. This is just one of many means that I will expose you to over time."

Doregos opened the briefcase with a lot of flourish, grabbed a bundle of hundred dollar bills and threw it on Disun's lap. "Here. Take that; go to Oxford Street; buy yourself some nice things; go out and have a great time tonight. Do whatever you need to do. Think about what I have shared with you. Let it sink. But keep this important question at the back of your mind: do you want to remain an ordinary pawn or do you want to be a player? You only have one chance. It is entirely up to you."

He paused for a moment and looked at the shell-shocked lad before him. "I am a little drained right now from all the meetings and travelling, so I need today to decompress. You may take your leave and get ready for a long day tomorrow."

"Okay, Sir. Thank you, Sir."

As Disun left, the money tucked in his back pocket, his mind began to race violently. Yet, his body moved slowly in a stupefied, zombie like fashion. He felt as though he had just been indoctrinated into a secret cult. What was he about to get into? His blood was pumping, his head throbbing. There were suddenly a hundred things to think about; a thousand possible ramifications. Yet, within all the complexity and flashing scenarios, one thing seemed constant, and every time his mind wandered in that direction, the complications seemed to whittle away, leaving a precise channel of clarity to a much-desired goal. It would take the whole day to ruminate and make sense out of his conflicting emotions. He certainly had neither the inclination nor the capacity for a shopping spree on the high streets of London.

CHAPTER 20

IN THE WEEKS AND MONTHS THAT FOLLOWED,
Disun submitted himself wholeheartedly to Dorego's tutelage. He became a fulltime apprentice of the latter's and, under his mentor's guidance, achieved even more recognition by moving lucrative client accounts from General Bank to Quorum, brokering complex deals internally and gaining more influence. Under Dorego's supervision, Disun commenced a full inquisition into the broad spectrum of extra-procedural bankers-clients' dealings, some borderline illegal and many fetching extraordinary financial rewards. These transactions – called *odu* – were off-the-record, often discussed in hush tones, after hours, or, as was often the case, away from the banking premises.

On the core banking side, one key prerequisite for career advancement – as Disun was quick to learn from his mentor – was the need for constant change and movement. According to Doregos, one way to guarantee regular progress within the banking industry was to move regularly from bank to bank on shrewdly negotiated terms, including multi-level promotions and exponential pay increase.

"You've got to understand that things heat up pretty quickly with the kind of transactions that go on in these climes," Doregos once said. "An important gift that every high-rolling banker needs to have is intuition. You have to know when you are being lined up for major recognition or when you are being set up for a disaster. There are no straightforward rules – just your intuition. And, perhaps to make things worse, the pattern of events precedent to both parallel outcomes is often similar. Both situations involve high-wire politicking; side meetings, after-hour rendezvous; backslapping and backstabbing. So, therein lies the great challenge: how do you differentiate one from the other, when the exact same scenarios could manifest in two distinct outcomes? But that also is where twenty years of experience and trained instincts come to play. The rule of thumb is that whenever in doubt, do yourself a favour: find the nearest exit. That way you are always one step ahead. As my mother always says, better safe than sorry. So, be prepared. Make good friends in the industry, have non-committal conversations with key players in various banks; engage with major head-hunters, albeit without anything that they could hold you on to; remain vague at all times, keep your options open."

By his twentieth year in the industry Dorego had changed jobs on six occasions. The changes came swiftly, with little warning and, without careful context, seemingly to the casual observer to be random, spur-of-the-moment decisions. But, as Doregos always liked to brag, there was a method to his madness. In all instances when Dorego had landed in a new bank, the change had inevitably come with much bigger, brand-new official cars, much larger offices, much fatter pay-cheques and more fringe benefits. And though the new positions had bigger job titles attached to them, it was always in a smaller bank. These promotions, therefore, in spite of the significant spike in benefits that came with them, did not necessarily come with an increase in the scope and scale of responsibilities.

"The smaller banks can be easily intimidated," Doregos was always fond of saying. "A promise to deliver the entire portfolio of deposit-bearing customers from your previous bank coupled with the dropping of a few big customer names is enough to get them salivating. In most cases, they had never received such huge deposits before in one swoop. They become yours afterwards. The good news is that once you join their bank and you deliver on your promise to any reasonable extent, they begin to see you as some sort of legend. At that point, you can get them to do your bidding. Just never let your guards down. Look powerful all the time and never miss the opportunity to remind them of the influential generals, governors and ministers that you have as friends and potential new clients. Let them know that you wine and dine with people that they only see on the pages of newspapers. Your aim is to own them. Once you do, you could, for instance, transfer your mundane workload to them. By doing this, you would have freed up more time for the deals. You would have thus created more time to play golf with the movers-and-shakers of the economy, while your colleagues are writing your dull credit reports back at the office. And these VIPs would respect you more for this, realising that you have enough flexibility and clout to play golf during business hours. By seeming to chose your own time; by coming and going as you wish, you will be demonstrating that you are in charge; one of the clique; a go-to guy. So they give you more deposits; more credit transactions. By taking this sublime position, therefore, you are quietly playing all sides and with a little bit of tact, and flare, this cycle of intimidation and subordination with your uninitiated colleagues would be sustained. Trust me, there is a method to this madness. You simply need to listen and learn."

Disun was somewhat baffled by Doregos' world-view. There was no question about that. But then, he had his eyes on the ball. If Doregos were the guru that he was proclaimed to be, then, he had better listen and learn as the guru had suggested. If there was anything else that he was fast learning from Doregos, it was to always separate yourself from the crowd. Nonetheless, he harboured a healthy respect for Doregos, now knowing fully well what the latter was capable of. If he were to be honest, this respect balanced delicately on the fringes of fear.

Within a short period, he had taken at least a dozen trips abroad with Doregos. Each trip came with its own unique destinations and innuendos. But of all the unusual experiences he had during his travels with Doregos, the memories of his first London trip, particularly, remained fixed on his memory. With Doregos' words randomly echoing in his conscience, he had returned to Nigeria after that trip, a changed man. He had been transformed, both in substance and in his sensibilities. Once he had overcome the magnitude of Dorego's revelations, and, mentally worked out the implications for his career and his life, assimilation had been easy. The result was a gradual but steady shifting of his ideals. A gradual but steady re-calibration of his essence. Nonetheless, he remained troubled by an abstract indiscernible feeling. Something that remained vaguely in his consciousness – ticking slowly away like an unpredictable time bomb – deeply unsettled him. This something was not unlike the vestige of an unnatural, life-altering experience; the witnessing of an abomination, for instance, or a sacrilege. It was the sort of deep-set knotty thing that psychologists are always trying to find; to define; to decipher. It was a little, amorphous something that set him apart from himself to the extent that he couldn't now boast with confidence anymore that he thoroughly knew who he was. He knew that Doregos' hotel-suite speech had something to do with this spiritual upheaval. Doregos had sown a strange seed in his psyche and, the more he evaluated it, the warier he was of the tree that would germinate therefrom.

Though this mental turmoil constantly snuck up on him, unannounced, and at random, he finally managed to set it aside and, on a subsequent trip, he found sufficient freedom to explore and enjoy London. Shopping on Oxford Street was unlike anything he had previously experienced – a materialistic high, it might be adjudged – and in the evenings when he returned to the hotel, Doregos would introduced him to the art of wine, cigars and fine dinning. Disun was fascinated by all these. He could really live this life, he thought one of the evenings, as he slouched on a sofa in Doregos' suite, trying to light a cigar while he waited for the latter who was getting dressed for the exclusive London nightclub that they had planned to conquer that night. By the time they had returned to Lagos, he was hooked on the high-rolling, lifestyle.

Today, he navigated his way through the myriad of narrow roads and alleys, which funnelled their pedestrian floods into Broad Street, not unlike the way capillaries would empty out their plasmatic contents into suctioning veins. Disun was feeling particularly good with himself this morning. His recent promotion at Quorum Bank came with benefits in excess of anything he had imagined when Doregos proposed this last movement to him. He was now a Manager in the Corporate Banking Department of the bank, with thirty-three officers reporting to him. Now that he had been schooled on the powers of money and now that he had developed a taste for material things, he couldn't seem to get enough. The industry placed a premium on glam: power dressing; power cars; and powerful head-office buildings and this reference to "power" subtly translated to ostentation. It became quickly clear to Disun that the more he embraced this culture of excessiveness, the more he was seen to be discerning, especially by the institutional leadership, which, essentially was all that mattered. Once you are liked by the powers-that-be, what else was important? And, the powers-that-be – as the banks' board and management were fondly called – could really make things happen for you. You could be invited to important Public Relations functions, even when you weren't senior enough in the hierarchy; and you would be asked to come along to powerful client meetings, just to simply enhance the visual landscape, even if all you would really contribute to the meeting was to take a few notes. Disun was comfortable with this silent prerequisite for acceptance. Money was clearly an additional impetus, and the more money he had at his disposal, the more he cultivated his fashion style. The response was reassuring. At six-foot-two, Disun wore a suit well, and with a physic that the Managing Director's secretary back at General once termed "refreshing", Disun literally had a strong structure to build on. Though he didn't know what to make of the secretary's comments, or her intent, Disun was appreciative, nonetheless. With new money flowing in, he was on a roll. Just that moment, as if by providence, the General Bank Head Office building came into view, and Disun allowed his imagination to wander for a second. What was the flattering secretary's intention, actually?

Quorum Bank's Head Office was still at least three blocks away, and when the pedestrian traffic got heavy – which it would on weekday mornings – Disun would drift back into the labyrinth of back roads for a block or two, just to get away from the slow-going corporate pedestrians, and salvage his punctuality goals. The quarter-hour trek from the commercial car park by the Marina – though seemingly hectic for an Armani-clad, high-flying banker such as himself – was inevitable. The parking facilities in most of the high-rise buildings on the Street were inadequate, and were usually reserved for the topmost executives and most important customers. This daily trek to and from the car-park was something that Disun cherished a lot; it was all the contact that he would have with the non-banking world – the *real* world – for weeks, and except for the odd weekend when he would steal a few hours to spend with his family at Makoko, he often went for months without a break in his routine. These walks had therefore progressed from a mere necessity to becoming the key highlight of his day, which, he now enjoyed.

The chance spectacles on the back routes connecting the Street were always rewarding. The other day, he came upon the Governor and his entourage, having apparently shown up to commission a new high-rise building. Then, one Saturday morning as he approached his office to catch up on his backlog of work, he was cut off by a winding procession of one of the traditional secret societies, men and women, clad in their one-piece, all-white shrouds, propped up by their two-meter long bamboo staffs as they trudged along, moving very much like a paramilitary regiment, but for their attires and the assortment of charms and amulets dangling from their necks and bare arms. Set against the background of simmering glass-and-aluminium skyscrapers, this unlikely spectacle could have been the outcome of carefully orchestrated contemporary artistry at the instance of a brilliant mind. Yet Disun knew that this was no art; it was reality, and as he waited for the procession to wear out, he found himself locking eyes with a number of the bare-chested, muscled young men, whom, not unlike him, seemed educated, sophisticated and well groomed. He felt that he recognised some of the members, but lacked the time and tranquillity to confirm. The closer he looked, the more he was confronted with the outward ordinariness of these people, and judging by the contemporary tattoo on a woman's arm, and what he perceived as the glitter of a diamond earring on a young man's ear, some of them were, actually, in all manners of the word, cosmopolitan. Then as he continued to contemplate these puzzling paradoxes of the Street – once the last had disappeared around a corner into the deeper crevices of the Island – he imagined what calculus had brought these people into the Society, knowing fully well that they could, potentially, be romanticizing with the occult. Inevitably, he found himself wondering about the nature of circumstances – for instance – in which he would yield to the allure of cultism and, perhaps rather more pertinently, if in any event that he did, how he would combine such an affiliation with his jet-setting life. Clearly, many of these people had no such conflicts; and if they did, nothing in their carriage and countenance suggested this. They seemed to have found for themselves an unusual formula that worked. They seemed eternally comfortable in their proudly bared skins.

Quorum was one of the New Generation Banks, having commenced business in the recent twelve years of the industry and having entered the industry even much later than the majority of its New Generation contemporaries. Quorum bank had the corporate equivalent of a sort of short-man complex, if there was anything like that. Everything that the Bank did had to be on a grand scale. The Bank's Head Office building could have been the tallest building on the Street and, perhaps in Nigeria had it not been shafted by the few meters worth of usurping mast at the pinnacle of the Union Bank building. With the dice cast, Quorum's

Managing Director – Mr Alonso Biobaku – had reluctantly succumbed to second place.

Disun had been quick to learn within the spate of a few months at Quorum, that while there are various corporate systems and structures on paper, the Bank's strategy was dictated, single-handedly by the Managing Director. Mr Biobaku was an unusual man in many respects. Many of his contemporaries perceived him a maverick, while a less-sympathetic section of the public saw him as a corporate cowboy. However, among this banking public was a crop of entrepreneurs and businessmen who flourished in the environment of induced flux that Quorum's anti-bureaucratic system provided, and this chaos, rather surprisingly – especially to his detractors – attracted a certain creed of customers in droves. With his maverick-cowboy persona, Mr Biobaku had managed to move the bank from its bottom ten ranking at inception, to top fifteen among the ninety banks in the industry based on its asset size. This transformation occurred within twelve quick years – a remarkable achievement by all standards – and while industry gossips were rife at the earlier stages of the Bank's operations, of far-reaching structural rot within its bourgeoning balance sheet, and while there had been occasional warnings of an imminent bust, Quorum Bank had survived against all the odds. With every year that the bank had opened its doors to customers, Mr Biobaku's brazenness and impetuosity had grown. Disun enjoyed the spontaneity that was the hallmark of the Bank's leadership, and whenever this translated into corporate drama, he even enjoyed it more. But the dramatic episodes were few and far between, and the most common manifestation of this strategy was rapid growth, which, in turn, played out in the scale and grandeur with which everything was done. Quorum Bank was larger than life and so was its flamboyant CEO, Mr Alonso Biobaku. Disun was confident that Quorum bank was the bank to be, and, at that stage in his career, being in such close interaction with the leadership of a major bank and their paraphernalia of office, he was like a shark that had caught the whiff of fresh blood. He was incensed.

Quorum was the stuff that high-flying dreams were made of.

Its marketing team included an army of gorgeous young women, who, upon close scrutiny could be fairly assumed to have been selected more for their physical other than professional qualities. Sitting in the banking hall, or at the bank's reception, these marketers would put on an inadvertent, military style-choreograph, walking back and forth with firm-strides amplified by the strike of their stilettos on marble, posture taut, eyes stern; brandishing their bosoms like bayonets – coarse, confrontational and controversy-courting. Among this creed, mini skirts had transcended fashion into the realm of necessity, and, it is a marvel to watch them tread in their six-inch stilettos, as a soldier would strut in boots. Still, not unlike soldiers, they deployed their natural endowment like tools, or, perhaps, more accurately, like weapons, since it had been said that "every tool becomes a weapon in the wrong hands" – indeed, in this case, weapons of man's destruction. With these young ladies, the worst-case scenarios often played out, whereby many an unsuspecting men would succumb, be conquered and, willingly tow a physiological leach into destruction, ultimately leaving their empires in ruins. These antecedents had been there throughout history: wars have been fought, fortunes dissolved, lives lost, and so it had continued up till today. It is nothing new and, perhaps, these high-rolling marketers see themselves as the custodians of a legacy – Cleopatras of our time. These were the secrete weapons of the banks, and, at Quorum, they were unleashed with reckless abandon.

At the highest echelon of this community of high-flying marketers was a young woman unlike any other that Disun had ever seen or known in his entire life – a young woman in her early thirties by the name of Abeni Asiwaju, or, simply, Benny, as she preferred to be addressed.

Benny was a quintessential corporate queen. Her mien betrayed a vibrant mind, peeking behind a veneer of ravishing beauty. And, as though beauty and brains were inadequate, Benny was gifted with uncanny brawn. It was not uncommon for her to be seen in public boisterous rumpuses with her colleagues and customers, just as easily as she could be seen engaging in fierce confrontations. Upon his first encounter with her, Disun postulated that her face must have represented for beauty what pheromones were for scents and her proportions – if they could be fairly referred to as that – were disproportionate, but rather in a charismatic way.

Perhaps what Disun found most alluring about Benny, was her movements. He could still remember the first time he saw her in the banking hall. He had just come into the bank that morning and was making his way to the counter with a cheque that he was eager to cash before he got engrossed in the day's work. He had turned the corner from the main entrance foyer, into the banking hall and had noticed a woman walking right in front of him. Her movements were unlike anything he had ever witnessed before then, fluid, semi-liquid, gelatinous. As he laterally followed in her footsteps, in what could only be described as a semiconscious trance, he realised that though her main aim – it appeared – was to move herself from one side of the room to another, there seemed to have been a clandestine – perhaps sinister – objective, as Disun was quick to decipher, – to knock the senses out of every man who had the plight or privilege of witnessing this act. While he tried to reclaim his mind from the gutters and focus on his original mission, it didn't take him long to comprehend that he was entirely at her mercy. As he watched her in front of him, his mind wandered for an eternal moment, and he could synchronise her movements with that of an equally endowed market woman, meandering within an unruly market crowd, fingers skilfully counting the proceeds of the day, an unrestrained tray of oranges balanced delicately on her head, trained feminine muscles twisting and twirling, in an intricate serpentine dance, as she strove, rather diligently, to sustain the balance of her load, while, at the same time, retaining the integrity of her unravelling wrapper, a feat that she would eventually accomplish, just through the mere wriggling of her waist. Disun had witnessed this montage of movements before, not once not twice, but on several occasions, and he knew with all certainty that such height of agility with complex muscular manipulation was never attained while plying the paved marble floors of banking halls. This level of proficiency could only come from constant manoeuvring in more rustic, marketplace situations, such as the one he had just imagined. To witness these instinctive movements underneath a shimmering cashmere skirt-suit within confines of a banking hall confused his senses for a moment, engendering a diabolical feeling of senselessness. Then he came back to a state of reckoning. This woman had been where he had been. They were from the same place. But then, who in the world was she!

He soon had the opportunity to obtain an answer as he settled beside her on the marble counter and tendered his cheque. He took a glance at her and noticed that her whole attention was focused on the cashier. Then after a few moments of interaction with his cashier, he took a second glance. He realised that while she wasn't exactly busy at that particular moment, she was studiously ignoring him. He thought he knew what exactly she was doing. She was deploying the classic snob tactic – and, boy, was she good! He played along for a while, but it wasn't long before his curiosity got the best of him. He seemed to have summarily lost all senses of restraint, and surprisingly even to himself, he had no apologies.

"Hi," he said, reaching out for a handshake. "I am Disun."

"Hi, Disun," she said, pausing momentarily, seeming to contemplate his hand, as one might a leper's, and then, finally taking it in perhaps the swiftest handshake that Disun had ever partaken in. Before he had the chance to react, she had turned her attention back to the cashier, and resumed her banking interactions. Disun was not lost on her failure to introduce herself; and, even more so, her seeming lack of further interest in him.

"My name is Disun." He reiterated, his tone emphatic.

"Benny," She volunteered eventually, neither flinching, nor turning to acknowledge him.

He smiled a knowledgeable, nonetheless awkward smile and returned to his cash transaction. He knew her type, he thought. Then, upon a second intuition, glancing at her as she maintained her regal, semi-athletic stance at the counter, eyes trained on the cashier, he reconsidered. Did he, really? Perhaps, he didn't. Benny was unlike anyone that he had previously known.

Her clean, delicate fingers tapped abstract rhythms on the marble counter as she waited for the cashier to process her request, her nails intricately polished in patterns of black, white and red, which, on the one hand was artistic, but on the other, perched perilously on the brink of gaudiness. Yet the shiny, spotty dots of *ina-ore* on the back of her hand, pointed to long-forgotten episodes of fire-play in a distant place where she must have dwelt in her adolescence innocent days. The dots left behind by the *ina-ore* – literally meaning the fire of friendship – bore forensic witness to a moonlight game played by children in further-flung places, or by newcomers to the city, who, stubbornly carried along their burden of egalitarian norms, and, often passed it on to the next generation. For many, back in the villages, *ina-ore,* and other games in its league, sustained well into the years of puberty, after which, for some, the flame of friendship would leap to the loins and the communal moonlight games would be circumvented by less chaste, pre-conjugal ballets.

As they continued to wait, the gentle breeze of the central air-conditioning brought the whiff of her perfume in his direction; yet, he didn't fail to notice the faint, but distinct tinge of camphor that free-rode on her perfume scent, betraying an entrenched culture that had endured in defiance of newly-found wealth. This vermin-resistance culture was familiar to him. Not unlike a prospect in a sales proposition, he was tempted to take a closer look, dropping his gaze below the counter, and then, further beneath the hem of the skimpy mini skirt. His exploration revealed taught, sculptured calves, adorned by a velvety smooth skin that paid tribute to years of pampering and good living. But upon a closer look, the residual scar of an *Okada* silencer testified to a branding mishap synonymous with patrons of the City's motorcycle transportation system, exposing humbler beginnings, or, recent-past. At the very base of this elegant mannequin, a covert war was being waged in the high-heeled shoes, as otherwise feral toes literally pushed back against an unadjusted life in confinement.

Disun was quick to interpret his findings. He was in full understanding. Benny was a hybrid, just like himself, and a relative newcomer to the glitz and glamour of the Street. While he could tell that Benny, just like him, was relatively new to the high-life in general, he could also tell that she hadn't arrived here by chance. Just standing there in close proximity, he could feel her aura, and the more he scrutinized her, the more the air at the back of his neck stood. As he grew older in life and progressed in his career, he was learning more and more from experience, that, in addition to sound logical construct, intuition was perhaps the most important decision-making asset that a man could have. The more he succumbed to this notion, the more he was learning to train and trust his instincts. If anything he had gained over the years was to go by, his gut feelings, that instance, was troubling. Benny's vibes were unsettling.

Disun's life experiences had taught him that men sought after women for various reasons. Most men would desire a soul mate at one point or another in their lives – someone with whom they could find a meeting of minds and share a quasi-spiritual coupling; this is the one that becomes the marathon-runner, home-keeper, care-giver, confidant. The wife. But then, some men also sought that prize; the trophy; something to flash and flaunt; something with which to oppress their peers – earn their respect, approval or envy. But then again, some men would aim to straddle both worlds, and in so doing, keep a mistress, or, even still, a second wife. Such were the ones who would jump into the treacherous world of bigamy and hope for the best; or opt for polygamy. However, all through the course of history, otherwise reasonable, self-respecting men had been known to have come into contact with a certain kind of woman – a woman that reeks only of pure sensuality – a woman, who, in many cases, would seem totally unlovable, given the intuitive knowledge that her essence was at the bequest of the highest bidder, and reasoning, therefore that they could never be the sole recipient. Yet, men had been known to have found such women irresistible – or so they had thought at the time – until such a time when, against their best judgement, they had succumbed, knowing fully well that their reputation, their livelihood and, even their lives could be in danger.

Something in Disun's mind screamed, *"obirin ajodi"*, referencing the scriptural "strange woman" of his half-hearted scripture-parleying days. This was a classic case. Yet, he continued to gaze at her; seemingly enthralled in the presence of the most attractive woman he had ever seen. As he pulled himself away from the counter, having received his cash and, thereby, concluded his transaction, he made a conscious decision in the innermost corner of his mind: for as long as they remained colleagues at the Bank, he would avoid Benny like a plague.

He didn't make good on his promise.

Serendipitously, their paths always crossed. And, as fate would have it – having heard of her drive and negotiation prowess – Doregos had invited her into his newly constituted high-powered marketing team. Consequently, Disun had had to relate with her much more than he would have envisaged. However, the more they interacted, the more he was astonished by how quickly his perceptions of her, and, indeed, his feelings towards her begun to change, even when this was rather to his own embarrassment. This unforeseen reaction towards Benny set him beside himself, and the more he struggled with his failings, the further he seemed to entangle himself. But then again, when he really thought about it, there was nothing particularly unusual in his ultimate reactions. Most men would respond to Benny in the same fashion.

Disun found Benny to be fiercely intelligent and on top of that raw intellect was a layer of wisdom that comes only from constant interaction with the elders or, in the alternative, constant exposure to complex shenanigans, often in semi-traditional, often polygamous extended family situations. Benny could go from fierce and fiery in one moment, to cunning and calculating the next. She could be daring and then, in the same breath, diplomatic, and sometimes as he watched her perform these intricate social ballads, his fascination would tether on the brink of fear. Who exactly was this woman?

Over and beyond everything else – at the end – his deepest allure derived from a fascination with her rough edges – those subtle rustic attributes – which only a co-traveller like himself could appreciate. He had continued to unveil new ones on every occasion; at every conversation; on every new day; and these, more than anything else, were those things which fully endeared him to her, because, after all said and done, they were from the same place. She had been where he had been.

Paradoxically, it was these same attributes that ruffled him. Knowing what he had endured to arrive where he presently was, he could but only imagine what *she* would have gone through. That earned her significant respect in his eyes; but if he were to be truthful, that respect came with a fair dose of fear. That fear, more than anything else, hinged on what he didn't know – the classic Donald Rumsfeld's *known-unknowns* – and it wouldn't have taken a soothsayer for him to have realised that there was a whole lot more to Abeni Asaaju than she was willing to let up; there was a whole lot more to her than met the eyes. Who really was Abeni Asaaju, and, more importantly, where had she been?

Abeni, for her part, left everybody guessing – perhaps realising the power of a little bit of mystic. However, the more Disun made it his mission to decode her, the more he was unwittingly spinning himself into her mystifying web.

CHAPTER 21

"ABEENI O!"

"Pscphew!" Abeni ignored her mother's bellow. Her reptilian hiss could have been audible in the next village. But it only seemed so in her ears, because if her mother had been privy to her insult, the latter would have had little remorse about putting an end to her flagrant, budding life. She smiled a self-satisfied smile, relishing her covet disobedience and the few more minutes that she had thus ascribed to herself while enjoying her solitary game of *suwe* before her mother would materialise in the backyard trembling with uncontainable rage, waving a life-threatening pastel in her hand, and promising to bring the whole building down. The old woman was getting tired from age, but also from the needless trouble that she put herself through on a daily basis – as Abeni often reasoned – and the former wouldn't rise from her near permanent position on her wooden bed-now-turned-couch until at least the third call.

"Abeniiiiiiiiiii!"

Abeni could hear the virtual barometer in her mother's voice turn up a notch. She giggled, then threw her little *suwe* placeholder – a symmetrical piece of reddish stone – into the target square in the six-box grid that she had drawn in the sand, then, she proceeded on a one-legged hop from one square to the other in her quest to recover the stone and edge closer towards victory in this preternatural one-man competition that she had set up for herself. Her *suwe* bore an imperceptible resemblance to the game that she played with her mother everyday, since, within her perception of the true scheme of things, her mother was technically just an element in the game, and, therefore, of little significance. At the end, her reaction or lack thereof, in any instance, to her mother's devices was entirely up to her, which, by implication, had become a conscious tension within her. Her response to her mother, was, as a result, almost always entirely at her discretion, and given her mother's incessant threats of violence such as might be witnessed at the end-of-the-world, her defiance had inevitably become a self-paced delicate game of will and defiance.

"Abeniiiiiiiiiiiiiiiiiii!!"

Abeni smiled, poised to cast her stone for yet another round. Then, as if struck by a sudden awakening, she remembered that they had a guest in the house, and, that, had automatically changed the dynamics of the contest with her mother. Her aunty – her mother's younger sister – had come in from Lagos that morning, and she was spending a few nights with them.

"Maaaaaa!" she yelled, as she dropped her *suwe* stone and hurried into the house. "Maaaaaaaa!" she yelled again, in a studied attempt at urgency.

"*Meeeeiiiiii!*" Her mother mimicked, making improvised mockery of her daughter's voice. "*Ori e o da!* You're counting my calls, *abi?*

"No Ma. I didn't hear you. I was at the backyard."

"*Ori e o da!*" Mama Abeni was getting old, and she had accumulated significant weight as the years progressed, impairing her movement and restricting her to her bed-couch most of the day. With her reduced mobility had come an increased dependence on Abeni and her sibling, and, to her chagrin, less agility to capture and punish her daughter whenever the latter was insolent. Feeling a compulsive need to control her daughter one way or another, she had traded her usual dexterity with slaps and pinches, for a versatility with spontaneous missiles – which essentially could be anything within arms reach – and when all failed, she would wholeheartedly resort to verbal abuse.

"*Oloriburuku…*" She yelled.

"*Sista mi,*" Abeni's Aunty – Sisi Eko – came into the room just at that moment, seeming astonished by her sisters' curses. "You have to watch what you say to these children, *Sista mi.* You shouldn't say negative things such as these."

"Is she your daughter?" Abeni's mother retorted. "You want to teach me how to raise my child?"

"I certainly can't teach you how to do that, *Sista mi*. You know I can't teach you anything for that matter. All I am saying is that there is power in pronouncements. And one should refrain from saying negative things, especially when it concerns one's own children."

"Well, keep teaching me, since you happen to know better than everyone else now. *Abi?* Now that you live in Lagos, what do village people like my humble self know? How can we even know how to train our own children?"

"Sista miiiiiii! You are completely going off in a different direction."

"Haaun!" Mama Abeni waved a dismissal hand. "Let us have nostrils to breathe. Lagos people. Thank God that we too have been there."

"Yes ma." Sisi-Eko's smile was in resignation. She knew not to prolong an argument with her sister, especially when the latter was consumed by her egotistic rage.

Abeni for her part was happy that Sisi-Eko's intervention had diffused her mother's anger and, even still, she was grateful that, for once, there was an alternate object of deluge for her mother's unending rage. She wondered how these new family dynamics would play out over the coming days.

"Iwo. You had better behave yourself." Mama Abeni wagged a menacing finger at her daughter, then after a pause, she dipped her hand into the small raffia basket beside her, and once she had rummaged through for a minute, produced a few rumpled Naira notes which she tried without success to straighten out. "Here. Go to the market and buy me some fish. Buy the dry ones from my friend. She knows what I want. Just give her fifty-Naira. Buy some salt and onions too."

"Yes, ma." Abeni collected the money and turned to leave, but she was stopped in her tracks by her mother's stern voice.

"And go and sleep there, if you want."

"No ma." Abeni had learnt to interpret her mother's sarcasm.

"What do I care? You know what awaits you if you do."

Abeni took her leave as Sisi-Eko started to warm up to her mother, seeking – as it seemed – to find a little sweet spot in her psyche to berth on, anchor and, with some luck, swing her mood and, hopefully, the overall atmosphere in the house. It was in her best interest to do so, in any case. Abeni didn't envy her aunt for the latter's inadvertent role, but, in a selfish corner of her mind, she was jubilant. She could share her burden with someone, for a change. Luckily, her mother harboured a similar resentment for her aunt, which, therefore, rendered the latter fair game.

Abeni eased herself into the village streets in the manner that an animal would ease into its natural environment. Ironically, the street was her home, since home – they say – is where an individual finds triumph. That Abeni found victory on the streets of Ifelodun was indisputable and as she eased into her street routine – adjusting her wrapper and recalibrating her steps – she gradually transformed into her subliminal role as the princess of the streets. In the same token, the streets welcomed her with open arms.

The journey to the market was uneventful, other than the whistling and yelling of the village boys as she went along – which, by then, had lost it's appeal and was becoming, for the most part, a nuisance. It wasn't long before she had claimed her prizes at the market and being that she had a unique abhorrence for market smells and spectacle, she wasn't one to linger on for a minute longer than was necessary. Within an hour, she was already on the way back home. The journey back home was just as boring – punctuated only by a near-mishap with her wrapper as she twisted and twirled along – but the more she shortened the distance to her house, the slower her pace became. Abeni bore a special disinclination towards getting home, and, if she were to be entirely honest, she would rather not have to return home in the first place. This was not a new feeling. This was a permanent feeling that she had, every time she left the confines of her mother's house and having to return to her perceived prison, after enjoying an hour or two of unalloyed freedom. If she had a choice, she would rather go somewhere else – and, if indeed she truly had a choice, she would abandon the house altogether. But, so far, she was bereft of alternatives; or, was she?

Well, upon second thoughts, she realised that she did have some options. At the minimum, she could defer her arrival at the house, for instance. She could gain a precious hour or two; find a story to tell her mother. Hopefully, the latter would be sufficiently distracted by her aunt to notice her absence; and even if she did, the worst result of her lateness was an avalanche of verbal abuse. She shrugged off the thought. Over time, she had become significantly insulated to her mother's insults to the extent that those alone were inadequate to deter her from doing whatever it was that she felt she needed to do at any point in time. This time, her mission was clear, and, having made a mental resolve; she was now with no other alternative but to follow through. At the next intersection, she turned off the market road and veered into a much narrower path that terminates – after fifteen minutes of brisk trekking down the line – at Sogo's bakery.

Once the dark shadowy silhouette of the bakery sprung up on the horizon and she could see the black puffs of smoke curling through the chimney into the open skies, her heart garnered momentum, and she could suddenly hear her pulse in her ears. She hadn't seen Sogo in several days, and she was excited that she was going to see him again, but she was also terrified by the unpredictability of her encounters with Sogo – which seemed to be veering into new dimensions in recent times – and the avalanche of nagging that she would have to endure once she returned home, should her mother eventually notice her prolonged absence. But then, what was life worth without taking an occasional risk? She only hoped that she could get Sogo to behave himself, this time.

The bakery ambience was, as expected, coloured by the tired market women and their wards milling around, dozing off, gossiping or doing whatever else that they did best, while waiting for Sogo to produce the next batch of bread. As usual, she was not lost on the furtive scoffs and rolling-of-the-eyes that accompanied her entry, being that by then, majority of the bakery community was now aware of the erstwhile clandestine rapport between their bakery mogul and his flame, who they now considered a deceptively innocent teenager. Their reservations not withstanding, they knew not to be openly critical of Sogo or his young aficionado, lest they should feel the full brunt of his reprisal, which, potentially, could result in an outright excommunication from the bakery. Sogo's bakery was a monopoly, and Sogo – being the shrewd entrepreneur that he was – was alert to his powers.

Abeni took a quiet place, knowing not to interfere with the bakery operations, and, at the same time, setting up for the expression of surprise that spontaneously leapt into Sogo's face whenever she showed up unexpectedly – an expression that she never seemed to tire of. Her favourite position was on a sawn-down log stool near the earthen oven area, which was partially hidden from the bakery crowd in the open hall and the workers by the oven, yet providing a clear line of sight – an almost panoramic view – to the entire bakery. This position would only be attractive to a loner and being that most of the bakery-goers liked to socialise – that being a fringe benefit of their bakery rendezvous – the position was almost always vacant. It had therefore inadvertently become a reserved space for Abeni, and, occasionally, Ologini, whenever she wanted a bit of solitude to snooze or groom herself. Abeni settled down on the improvised stool, set her ware carefully beside her, curled up against the rustic earthen wall in that section of the building and immersed herself in the collage of stimuli in the bakery.

It wasn't long before Sogo materialised in his traditional work uniform, covered in what seemed like a decade's worth of soot and sweat, which ordinarily should radiate a repulsive pong, but which, rather unexpectedly only effuses an alluring pastry scent, having, as it seemed, been kept sanitary over the year by constant exposure to the smoke and blistering heat of the oven. As always, Sojo stopped right in his tracks, and his entire face glowed with the intensity of his oven, right before he slid in the first trays of risen dough.

"Ah, Abeni. I didn't know you were here."

He went over to her, and stood around for a moment; smiling, speechless; intermittently wiping the sweat that was tricking down his temple with the sleeves of his uniform. "You need some bread?"

She shook her head; remained silent and maintained the stern, colourless expression with which she mellowed him down.

Okay. I see. Just visiting, then?"

She nodded, still silent.

"Okay. I will be with you in a moment. Just make yourself comfortable."

Sogo disappeared as he had appeared, only to reappear within a short while with a small parcel in his hand – something wrapped up in old newspapers – and handed it to Abeni.

"You can keep busy with these while I finish with the batch in the oven. The stuff in the oven is the last batch for the day, so I am just about ready to wrap up."

Abeni opened the newspaper wrappings to reveal a fresh loaf of bread. "Thanks," she said, her manner coy, yet, at the same time, alluring.

Sogo pulled a gracious smile. "You know where to find water." He began to take his leave. "Make yourself comfortable. I will be back once I am done."

Abeni nodded in silence as she tucked into the bread while Sogo vanished once again into the interior of the bakery. She watched from her vantage spot as the bakery trade unfolded before her eyes, not unlike a well-rehearsed dance. Once the bread was baked to perfection, the simmering bread trays were retrieved by the bare-chested bakery boys, four or five trays at a time, and set on the bare floor which now maintained a dark shiny gleam, acquired over a dozen years on grinding and polishing from the trays and baking fat. Almost immediately, they were organised ten to twenty trays at a time and slid right across the floor to yet another corner of the bakery, where they were arranged in an orderly pattern, resembling an aberrant square-honeycomb. Subsequently, the trays were upturned unto long sheets of newsprint spread across the floor while another of the bakery hands arranged them according to their respective sizes and quality. At that point, the buyers swarmed around jostling for the perfect size, quantity and quality mix.

Abeni immersed herself in this spectacle for a while, which she still found entertaining, even when she had witnessed it over a hundred times. It wasn't however long before it lost its charm and she begun to worry about making it back to the house on time. Every so often when Sogo scuttled by in search of change for a customer or to fetch old newsprint-wrappings for a testy buyer, or to run any one of the half-dozen odd errands that he ran during the selling shift, Abeni would throw him a quick forlorn look, and every so often, ramp this up a notch by feigning anxiety, to which she would elicit the same cool calm and collected response from Sogo, entailing the gentle and continuous wiping of his palm down his sweaty chest in a classic "calm down" expression. This routine of action and reaction – panic and pacification – continued for another half hour, until the last of the bakery customers was gone, and until, finally, the last of the bakery hands had been dismissed. Then, Sogo came to her, pulled a small stool and sat beside her.

"I am so sorry, Abeni. These people: they always want my blood."

Abeni rolled her eyes, unimpressed. "Keep pretending. Who doesn't know that you thrive on their attention and money?"

Sogo smiled a sheepish smile. He was one to be easily caught in a tongue-tied corner of discomfiture. "Well, sorry for keeping you waiting."

"Sorry won't cut it, Sogo. I am already in serious trouble. My mother would kill me."

"Don't worry, Abeni. She wouldn't. She probably doesn't even realise that you've been away for so long. Besides, you are not a child anymore, Abeni. Your mum needs to start getting used to that."

"I am still a child, Sogo. I am just eighteen."

"You are not a child, trust me," the expression on Sogo's face changed. "You are a woman."

Abeni smiled, embarrassed. Vanity has become a vice that she had very little means to control. Sogo knew how to capitalise on this.

"And a very beautiful woman at that." He paused, his eyes groping her in the dim light of the bakery. Then he stretched out his hand and held hers, gently, gingerly. "You are a very beautiful girl, Abeni, and I want to take very good care of you. When the time comes, I will come and meet your mother. I would let her know how I feel."

Abeni let out a nervous yelp that was intended as a laugh. But she was, in actual fact, overwhelmed by Sogo's pronouncements. "You can't be serious. You don't know my mother. She would kill you."

"And who says that I am not ready to lose my life because of you, Abeni."

Abeni's discomfiture came through in her reticence. She dropped her gaze to her feet. "Well, I need to go now, Sogo. My mother is waiting for me."

"*Ha-haaan,* Abeni. Don't be in a hurry, now." He squeezed her hand softly. "Do you want to leave me here by myself? Okay, just spend a few more minutes."

Abeni did not volunteer a response. She merely sat there, batting her eyes.

"Besides, I have a little special something for you." Sogo's wink was conspiratorial. "I know you're getting tired of my bread gifts, so I arranged something different. I have some change for you."

The sound of money gave Abeni's heart a kick. Materialism was only second to vanity among her emerging vices and given that her mother was – by her definition – the stingiest woman in the world, Sogo's proposition was good tidings to her ears. She snatched her hand from Sogo's and tendered her palm before him.

"Okay, let me have it. I have to hurry back now."

"*Haba...*Abeni. Not so quickly now." Sogo wagged a gentle negating finger. "The money is in my office. Come with me."

"You go and get it." Abeni was not lost on the silent condition to Sogo's gift promise. She knew the so-called office. It was a small protrusion on the side of the building. Something that Sogo quickly put together as a retreat from the production and storage operations of the bakery. Sogo's office, in spite of its protagonists fancy descriptive, was, in actual fact, a sparsely furnished shack. "I will wait for you here."

"My dear Abeni. Eh? *Idi-Ileke,*" Sogo's face had by now acquired a lost, earnest expression. It was a new expression and Abeni was witnessing it for the first time. She could tell that he was mentally on his knees. "Don't neglect me..."

For the next few seconds, Abeni contemplated her options.

She had been in the back office with Sogo a number of times before, and it was nothing unusual that he was prompting her again today. There was however something in his expression just that moment that seemed a bit different. There was a sharp, determined, almost animalistic glint in his eyes, and while she believed that she held his numbers and knew how to influence him to do exactly whatever it was that she wanted, something seemed a bit different that evening. Her disquiet could have been based on fact, or it could have just been a premonition. Whatever it was, she just didn't feel as comfortable as she usually would have been in acceding to Sogo's request. It could also have had to do with her inevitable lateness in returning home and concerns about her mother's reaction when she eventually did. She was therefore very anxious about lingering on longer in Sogo's bakery, let alone opening a new chapter of the evening by following him into the back office.

On the other hand, she knew just how generous Sogo could be, especially when he wanted something from her and was as giddy as he presently was. Her memory of the last "change" that she received from him was fresh, and she could still remember how she spent every Kobo of the windfall on nick-knacks. Faint traces of the banquette of flavours from the *taba-taba, kuli-kuli, chuku-chuku, panbola-bola, chin-chin and* all the *other* sweet things that she had routinely selected from the provisions vendor's rack still clung to her taste buds, tingling at her nerves from time to time. In a moment of distraction, she wondered why these homemade sweets had such whimsical names, with even the large manufacturers jumping on the oxymoronic bandwagon with their own *goody-goody* and *tom-tom* sweets. Then, she wondered why some had deviated from these trends, only to conceive even stranger gimmick of their own, with curious brands such as *President Gowon's fingernails* and *lizard's eggs*. And while the jury was still out on the superiority of one branding trick over the other, there was no dispute as to what Sogo's cash handouts could do in facilitating a fresh cache of goodies.

This momentary detour down memory lane was all that was necessary to sway her, such that when Sogo got on his feet, held her hand and pulled gently, she yielded. As they made their way through the bakery to the back-office shack, Abeni's mind was ravaged by a complex calculus that strove, rather rigorously, to weigh Sogo's promise of an imminent bounty against the carnage that would await her upon her return to the house. Her entire body trembled with a unique blend of fantasy and fear.

"Don't worry, ehn, Abeni; *Idi-ileke*. Everything will be alright."

When they emerged from the back-office half-an-hour later, Abeni was agitated and anxious to leave. She didn't have a watch, but a quick glance at the rusty clock on the bakery wall showed that it had been four hours since she had left the house. She knew that she was in trouble on a scale that was hitherto unknown to mankind, but she was hopeful that if her mother went on a rampage, her aunty would be on hand, and willing, to intervene. Whatever happened, she would have Sogo's Naira gifts, rolled up in her wrapper, to fall back on. She prayed quietly in her mind. Things could spiral out of control when she got home. Then, as she approached the makeshift stool where she had kept her belongings, she was met with a scene that sent shock waves down her entire being. The scream that leapt out of her mouth could have emanated from the deepest bowels of hell.

"Yeeeeeee! I am dead!"

"*Ologiniiiiiiii…!* You crazy witch!" Sogo charged forward in rage, grabbed a broom and swiped savagely at his cat. He missed and before he could regroup for a second attack, the cat was already among the struts and noggins of the naked roof, looking down at them with what seemed like giggly, cynical eyes.

By then, Abeni was scrambling on all fours, trying frantically to re-assemble her ware. Ologini had scattered her groceries all over the bakery floor, and, to her chagrin, she had dug in considerably into one of the fishes.

Abeni let out a melodic tune of pure pain. "Ologini has killed me o!"

"This stupid, crazy witch!" Sogo fumed. "I will kill you today!"

Sogo's bid was earnest, frantic, and it was likely that if indeed he had been able to get a hold of Ologini – his long-time friend and companion – he would have taken her feline life. But, as fate would have it, Ologini was gifted with a nimbleness that was alien to all men, and, incidentally, Sogo, in spite of his anger, was still human. As Ologini watched with bright vigilant eyes from a dark corner within the canopies of the bakery, Sogo attempted to console his lover.

"It's okay, Abeni. It's not the end of the world."

"Ah, Sogo. That's coming from your mouth? You have killed me today. You and your stupid devil-cat."

"I'm sorry, eh? *Idi-ileke.* If only I had known that you had fish in there. Ologini cannot be trusted."

"Just shut up and stop talking." Abeni clambered to her feet and arranged her wrapper. "Just shut up. Your speech cannot help me now. I have to organise my thoughts."

She claimed her wares and headed for the door. Sogo maintained a close distance. "I'm so sorry, Abeni…"

"Shoooosh! Please, please, please…"

On getting home, Abeni was met with the full brunt of her mother's tongue. The verbal exchange was fluid and the abuse rained down on her like an acid storm. The bone of contention all the while had been her lateness, but that was only until her mother noticed the bone sticking out meaningfully from her cherished fish. From that point onwards, it was pandemonium in the household. As though possessed by a new, agile demon, Mama Abeni pulled herself from the bed, scampered into the out-door kitchen and returned looking inflamed, brandishing a dirty scapula in her hand. Fearful of a dire outcome, Sisi-Eko stepped in, scrambling to get in her sister's way and prevent her from reaching Abeni where the latter crouched in a corner, awaiting the impending maternal blight. But Sisi-Eko – all fifty-five kilograms of skin and bones – was no match for Mama Abeni on an ordinary day, let alone in her present state of enthusiasm. With one swing of her fat arm, Mama Abeni shoved her hapless sister to one side of the room and, upon arriving at her daughter's corner, unleashed her own version of Armageddon.

The following morning as she made to leave for Lagos, Sisi-Eko went to bid her niece goodbye. She found Abeni curled up on a mat in her bedroom, in a foetal position, bruised, battered and barely awake.

"Abeni …"

Abeni hardly responded; neither did she move. Sisi-Eko entertained a few moments of apprehension, but struggled to remain calm.

"Abeni," she tapped on her niece's back gently. "Abeni, I'm leaving."

"Okay, Aunty."

"You scared me for a minute. Here. This is my address in Lagos. If your mother ever goes crazy on you like that again, or if for whatever reason you have any concerns about your wellbeing, find some money and come to me in Lagos. I am in two minds about doing this, but I also feel responsible."

Abeni's response was indistinct. She seemed confused, incoherent. With unsteady hands, Sisi-Eko gathered her things and, without further ado, tiptoed out of the room.

BOOK III
LAGOS, 2000S

CHAPTER 22

NOTHING PLEASED DISUN MORE than his occasional visit to Makoko. Through the years, these had become integral to his psychological balance and even though his visitations had become fewer and further-between, as time went on, they had nonetheless remained important dates on his calendar.

As a rule, a trip to Makoko would be pencilled down for that rare day-off on a public holiday – since normally, he treated public holidays as regular working days – or on that opportunistic occasion when he would wrangle a day or two out of his annual leave, prior to taking an overseas trip. Mini-pilgrimages – he called these Makoko trips – something to get him grounded. Not that he was ever far away from his roots, in any case, and despite his ascension to the pinnacle of his carer on Broad Street, he had never lost touch with who he was. While he had an appreciation of how far he had come, he maintained a keen sense of where he was coming from. It did help that his twenty-fifth floor corner office with its three-meter high all-glass curtain walls provided a direct line of sight to Makoko – albeit barely – presented as a three-foot peek between the jagged maze of competing concrete and glass structures. Whenever the weather was clear and there was reprieve from the constant smoke bellowing out of the rows of archaic sawmills by the lagoon, the view, as ghastly as it may seem to an outsider, was, as Disun often found, soothing. But then, even on the worst days, when the view was usurped by weather, smoke, a conspiracy between both, or, simply, the descent of dusk, he would resort to the large oil portrait of Broad Street hanging dead centre on one of the solid walls in his sprawling office. While the painting offered a reverse perspective – depicting Broad Street from a point at the edge of the Lagoon, somewhere in Makoko – it elicited a similar emotion in him. The fact was that this portrait often drew out an even stronger emotion, since it always took him back to a place and time, decades earlier, when he would sit on the ramshackle deck of a dilapidated shack with his friend, Ige, and contemplate the prospects of life on the *other side*. He yielded to a fleeting smile, remembering the artist's reaction when he had described his vision of the painting that he was about to commission.

"I want the portrait to be dark, grim, hazy… and I want the buildings of Broad Street rising out of a hazy cloud of smoke."

"Well, that's rather interesting, Sir, but I would have thought the portrait might look even more exciting against a clear foreground, say on a bright, sunny afternoon." The young artist had been slightly nervous, yet, assertive.

"Well, isn't that the essence of art? It's all about context; perspectives. In the end, I have a certain vision for the painting, and I think the foggy scenario best captures this. I'm sure you can deliver on this vision."

"I'm sure I can, Sir."

"Thank you."

Disun usually enjoyed a good debate, and, his natural tendency would have been to engage the artist further on his reasoning, present a fair argument of his own and have a healthy, intellectual discussion until the superior argument prevailed. But then, how would he have explained to the youth that his perspectives of the Street, sitting on those platforms many years ago, had not only been tainted by the fog drifting along from the adjacent sawmills, but also, by the pungent cloud, emanating from Ige's custom fag, which, perhaps was the most pertinent influence, since it did not only colour his vision of the Street, but also his intellectual posture. How do you discuss something like that with a bright-eyed, pure-hearted, nineteen-year-old kid?

He found himself giggling to himself. Ige – what a guy!

But then, still, there was no better reality check, other than to climb down from his lofty twenty-fifth floor office from time to time, and a drive down to Makoko – which could be easy or harrowing, depending on the time of day, or day of the week, or both – and, ultimately, a leisurely stroll down the streets and alleys. Even, beyond that, nothing beat the constant expression on his mother's face whenever he arrived at the door; that expression that ordinary words would try, but inevitably fail, to describe. This expression itself was at the very centre of this periodic trip. This, he would often imagine, was an expression that every parent should have the privilege of enjoying, if only once in their lifetime.

Disun smiled quietly to himself once again.

He recalled how Angela – his hyper-efficient secretary – had popped her well- groomed face through the door that morning and interrupted his reverie. Angela was one of those women who could be described as intensely beautiful, yet in a way that was stark, pure, and bereft of any form of pretentiousness. Angela's beauty effused wholesomeness, and so did her mind. She was preternaturally different from the stereotypical banking femme that surrounded him, and for all her qualities, Disun held her in high esteem.

"Sir, a gentleman came in with a note earlier in the morning," she had said. "I actually left it on your desk, but I guess you may not have noticed it among the myriad of correspondences." She approached his endless desk and retrieved a small brown envelope underneath a stack, flapping it playfully. "See, I can see it's already buried beneath all the other stuff. According to the folks at the reception, he mentioned that it was very important. That it was from a certain Mr Olukayode."

Debo froze for a moment and gave Angela his whole attention. "Mr olukayode? Which Mr Olukayode is this?"

"I think he also mentioned that the sender is an old friend of yours."

Disun had seemed baffled for a fleeting second, then the grin that wreathed his face was full. It was Ige, after all. That much he was able to confirm without further doubt once he opened the envelope. Ige's flowery calligraphy was inimitable:

Hey, Disun. I am in town for a couple of weeks. I understand you are now a very big boy. Well, I am not surprised. Olumide told me where to find you. But then, I choose not to give you a shock. I'm in Makoko, for now. Flamingo Hotels. Whenever you have some time.

-   Ige Gabrielle Olukayode (0217 534 3374)

Whenever you have some time? Really? Ige must have become a joker! Disun grabbed his mobile phone and, with his forefinger poised like a woodpecker's beak, feverishly punched out Ige's number. Then, as the phone was about to connect on the other side, he cut it off. It was of no use. Of what purpose was it to be speaking to Ige over the phone without seeing his expressions, grabbing his neck if need be; maybe throwing a few amiable punches. Making this first contact over the phone, several years on, wouldn't cut it. From that moment onwards, Disun had been unable to focus on his agenda for the day.

Recently, Disun had come to accept wanton frustration as an inevitable by-product of a driving expedition on Makoko Main Road. Somehow, the same road that was fearfully wide when he was growing up in the neighbourhood seemed to have shrunk over the years, to the point, in recent times, where it had narrowed into a mere alleyway. Though this transformation could sometimes seem mysterious, upon closer examination, it wasn't difficult to detect the combined causes of the lock-jam. At first, was the slow creeping-growth action of the stores adjourning the road, deploying their shelves like non-retractable wooden proboscises, growing by a foot or two a year and mimicking a one-way tide, as they pushed the lines of *omolanke* carts, *Okada* bikes and pedestrians further and further into the road. Typically, indiscriminate parking on either sides of the road would aggravate this already tense reality, and it didn't help that Disun was being chauffeured, for the first time on this occasion, in a much larger vehicle than he customarily would have. This unregulated race-to-the-bottom would continue, unperturbed, until a big Government official would need to navigate this chaos to a publicity-seeking ceremony, and the local government crew, in advance of the event, would, in an induced moment of dignity, hurry to clean up the mess. As it wouldn't be any other way, the race to the centre of the road would summarily resume, unabated, once the excitement of the government stunt had subdued.

As there hadn't been a big-government entourage traversing the area in five years – at least not in any covert, official capacity – the road was at the height of it's cyclical narrowing. Disun's driver was having a particularly difficult time manoeuvring the Mercedes Benz through the tense mix of parked car, pushcart and pedestrians, and, against his inherent tendencies, Disun had learnt restraint, studiously resisting the role of back-seat driver. However, the more he watched the charged interactions between his driver and nearby road users, the quicker he understood why the tension seemed particularly high this afternoon. It was two weeks to Christmas. Of course!

In Makoko, Christmas – just like all other religious festivities – was accompanied by extraordinary fanfare. The key distinction, however, was that Christmas coincided with the end of the year. This year-end celebration offered the hard working population a chance to display how successful their working year had been. The vast majority of Makoko residents were natives of towns and cities outside of the Metropolis and many who could afford the transportation fare to the village and the necessitous budget for gifts and expenses would travel during the festivities. Those who couldn't wished that they could, and, in many cases, would work extra hard towards the last few days, hoping that they could salvage their travel plans. As the days drew nearer, the tension would increase. Traders would take full advantage of the anxiety and excitement, as would thieves, and this corrosive, zero-some game would continue until the very end. In the early, idle days of the New Year, many would share tales of glory; yet, most would have gory tales to tell, or as was often the case, ruminate in private. In the meantime, everyone participated in the moment. The following year, and, indeed, the following decade would take care of itself.

Once the Benz was parked at an opportunistic spot on the road, Disun and his driver commenced the long trek through the myriad of alleys and corridors to his father's new house. Suddenly, Disun's heart acquired new momentum. Recently, the demands of his new role as Executive Director at Quorum had made it difficult to keep up with his routine visits to see his family. He entertained a moment of guilt, but then, he found solace in his subsequent thoughts. His fight for prosperity had equally been for their sake, and, to be candid, he had been fair. The two-storey house that the family now occupied was built entirely with his money, though the title was in his father's name and he always ensured that the old man was at the forefront during the construction period. The new house, sitting on a full plot of reclaimed land – a rarity in Makoko – towered above the sea of tumbling shacks all around it, thus commanding a generous view of the Lagoon. Relocation to the new house had earned the family respect and pride, and whenever he saw his father standing tall on the second-storey balcony, smiling down at him as he approached, his eyes would gather some mist.

His arrival protocol involved a ten-minute rendezvous with the dozens of neighbourhood kids who would waylay him at the gate, having been notified by an advanced squad from the main road. Since he now enjoyed a hero status among the youth, Disun had learnt to respect and cherish that privilege, ensuring – based on a silent code evolved over the course of his many visits – that he would only proceed into the house after he had summoned their leader and parted with a generous wad of currency. During the festive seasons, the youths would expect him to make a contribution towards their carnival expenditure. This time, however, in addition to the carnival budget, he had resolved to embark on a further-reaching community project for the youth; something he had been contemplating since the beginning of the year.

The next stage involved a few more minutes at *Opening-Soon* the convenience store occupying most of the building's ground floor. The store's name was derived, accidentally, from the tiny red-and-white sign that was nailed to the door two weeks prior to it's opening, while the family awaited Disun's return from his overseas trip to deliberate on a suitable name. At the end, the customers elected this temporary identity, and regardless of the owners' opinion afterwards, *Opening-Soon* stuck. The family knew better than to argue with their customers, and, seizing a rare branding opportunity, they kept it. Olumide ran the store with his mother, and it provided the family with a steady income. It also provided Olumide with a safe and sustainable career, given his condition. *Opening Soon* had become the de-facto convenience store for the neighbourhood, if not the entire community, and Disun could not help but notice the pride on Olumide's face whenever someone called him "Manager" as they travelled through the area streets.

It was two weeks to Christmas! Of course! And, the mood in the atmosphere drove this home. From the roadside stores busting at the seams with gaudy decorations, to the half-dozen fragile CD-Players in every alley, spewing out Christmas rhymes, not to mention the street traders vying for brisk business with their every rancorous call and the near-panicky sense of urgency charging the air.

All across the neighbourhoods, the heart-jolting shatter of a thousand firecrackers rend the air, bringing Disun fond memories. The firecrackers of choice were the imported *knockout* or *banger* brands from China, but being that these were out of the reach of the vast majority, the ghetto ingenuity once again kicked in and came through. Makoko kids had been known to have forged bespoke firecracker devices out of bicycle spokes, filling the hollow tips with shaved-off match-heads, plugging this up with a snug nail and setting off an explosion with a decisive rack against a concrete wall. A variation of this device was achieved with the sawed-off cylinder of a spent *champion* spark plug, driven into a wooden handle and let off with the same racking-of-plugged-in-match-head-shavings-against-a-concrete-wall action. A daring few worked with even bigger tools, consisting of improvised metal cones forged out of rusty car engine parts, aiming to summon an even louder explosion. Yet, an audacious elite gang would forage into the local vulcanizers' dens in the depth of the night to pilfer rare white carbide salts with which they fomented the mother-of-all-explosions, which they would summon when the volatile fizzes of the smouldering salt found flame.

Most mothers watched and listen in horror as the explosions went off, one after the other. An unlikely alliance of hostile fathers and sullen, previously robbed vulcanizers, engage in a game of cat-and-mouse, chasing the villains from one hidden corner of the ghetto to the other and rending the air with their own evenly explosive curses. In defence of their actions, the kids labelled their material-grabbing antics as "salvaging", or "surplus skimming", a viewpoint that they often sustained until they fell foul of a vigilant artisan and were made to bear the full brunt of their misadventures. From all angles, this was a dangerous game; but, true to type, the ghetto boys played wholeheartedly, downgrading the magnitude of their vice and fulfilling their seasonal addiction to explosions, in defiance of their parents, and, as it seemed, everyone else. As one might expect, these improvised explosive devices malfunctioned every now and then, sending metallic and ceramic shrapnel in all directions, many of which found unprotected skins and muscles, leaving ghastly mosaic scars as life-long testimonies of youthful exuberance. Some of Disun's adolescence friends were reported to have had near-blinding experiences, and some were rumoured to have ceramic shrapnel permanently imbedded in their shins.

As the explosions resonated in quick successions all around the area, and as the much younger children erupted in celebration with each bang, a small group among the adults looked on with quiet approval. The children's applause and laughter seemed to ease the daily pressures, if only for a moment, and in these acts of defiance, some relived an era of fearlessness and grit; a period in their lives now long abandoned; long gone.

Disun finally accessed the house, and after a half-hour of his arrival routine, he was pleased to finally walk into his mother's embrace. Olumide came upstairs with him and their intermittent conversations picked up from where it had last stopped. Baba and Mama Disun had learnt to leave them alone, whenever they got caught up in their vibrant talk. At some point, Olumide digressed into the affairs of the shop, and, without being aware, begun to render some mental accounts. Disun raised a quick, negating finger.

"You know how we do this, Olumide. The shop is your business – your responsibility. I have no interest in getting into your affairs."

"It's *our* business, Disun. But I get your point. I certainly do."

"For sure, Bro. Manage it well, and take care of the folks. That's all I ask of you. I have absolutely no doubt in your abilities."

"For sure, Bro."

An hour later, Disun shared a meal with his family, and then set out for Flamingo Hotel.

Flamingo Hotel was set in the better district of Makoko, close to the police station and the Total petrol station serving the area. The police station's vast junkyard of rusting seized cars and the petrol station's drive-in complex provided a rare sense of space in that area, leaving a mini oasis of relative sanity in Makoko's densely constructed jungle.

Disun proceeded to the reception, his driver close behind him. The gangly, seemingly uninspired woman manning the reception paid scant attention to her guests as she scribbled away into a large register. As bad as the prevailing customer service tradition was across the city, Disun had learnt to tone down his expectations even further, whenever he was at the archetypical epicentre of this decadency, which couldn't be better exemplified anywhere else than in places such as Makoko.

He ventured an attention-drawing cough as they arrived at the worn reception desk.

"Evening, Madam."

"Good Evening, Sir," The gangly receptionist said, finally realising, at that point, that she had run out of leeway with the routine shirking of her duties. "What can I do for you, Sir?"

"I'm here to see Mr Olukayode… Ige Olukayode… I understand that he is lodging here."

"Yes, Sir. Mr Ige is putting up here. He is actually at the garden bar at the moment. The bar is behind the building, through that small passage. If you don't mind, I can lead you to where he is, Sir." Being her sole concept of etiquette, her intermittent "Sirs" were fast and frequent.

"Thank you."

The receptionist shoehorned herself from the back of the front desk and led her guests across the room through a series of short passages into an open space at the back of the building. Bordered on all sides by the hotel building and the compound walls, the space seemed more like a courtyard than a garden, and the scarcity of greenery put paid to this fact. Smack in the middle of this open space, were a few clusters of garden tables and chairs, many of which were occupied by couples caught up in romantic reverie and a few unaccompanied women, moping around with a rather suspicious mien. To the right hand side of this crowd, set against the raspy bare-concrete wall, a Suya chef executed his trade, filling the air with aromatic fumes of singeing onions and spices; and to his left, an energetic deejay effused an eclectic sequence of rhythms from his turntable.

At the centre of this garden rendezvous, a small crowd gathered around a table, surrounding a man whom clearly was the centre point of their attention. The crowd seemed out of place, their appearance giving them up as visitors rather than residents of the area. Three men stood like sentries around the table, all wearing blue jeans, white shirts and dark coloured blazers. At the table, an athletically built, bald-headed man sat, dangling a half-burnt cigar between his fingers, a diamond ring on his pinkie catching the light as he did. The young lady sitting next to him was deathly quiet, playing with the wineglass before her and seeming disinterested in the men and their discussions.

As Disun and his driver drew nearer to the crowd, they caught a better glimpse of the man in the middle. The athletic bald man, appeared to be in his late thirties, clean-shaven, well groomed. His black blazer, unlike his minders', was of designer quality, and he had jewellery peeking from every square inch of exposed skin. He sat with a confident, accomplished air, and as he spoke, the men around him tendered their rapt attention. Though this new appearance of age, wealth and power was momentarily distracting, Disun knew exactly who this charismatic maestro was. It was Ige.

"Ige ... *Ogbologbo* ," Disun reached out to grab his friend by the nearest piece of flesh or fabric that his hand could touch, but, then, as if withheld mid-action by a pneumatic crane, he was seized by four powerful hands and gently set two paces backwards on his feet. Disun was frantic and as he wriggled and shrugged to free himself, and, just as his driver prepared to react, the minders offered an expert cocktail of apology and coercion, causing him to reconsider. Ige made to intervene, and as he got on his feet, the glow of recognition illuminated his face.

"Disun! Disun *Baba*!" He begun to manoeuvre his way around the table, and, seeing his reaction, his minders retracted from Disun and backed away slowly. "Disun. "

The ensuing embrace was chaotic; near violent. As the men locked together laughing with gusto, backslapping, neck grabbing and whispering inaudible jargons into each other's ears, the entire gathering in the garden looked on with mesmerised eyes. As the duo interacted, all airs of accomplishment and big-men etiquettes were summarily lost. In this extraordinary moment of reunion, the embracing duo was back to where they had left off. They were no more than the fraternal ghetto boys that they used to be.

That evening, Disun did not leave the Flamingo Hotel until well after midnight. Their re-bonding hours were very well spent, with each eager to catch up on what the other had been doing. Other than his leaner, meaner muscles and a few signs of aging, Disun realised, rather to his surprise, that ten years down the line, his friend had not changed that much. However, materially, Ige couldn't have been any further away from the teenage kid that he knew back in the neighbourhood. By all accounts, Ige had grown into a fine, granted colourful, gentleman. Disun had a feeling that the latter was having the exact same thoughts about him.

After the initial excitement had worn down, Ige introduced his entourage: the three bodyguards which he had brought along with him from the States, all American nationals – with the exception of their leader, Dede, who was a naturalised American of Nigerian descent – and Loretta, an American woman of Caribbean heritage whom Ige introduced as his Executive Assistant but who seemed slightly too close and casual with her boss to have been keeping strictly to her job description. Disun introduced his driver – Gbola – who, in spite of his job title, was a fifth-Dan karate black-belter and an expert at armless combat.

By all indications, Ige had come into a lot of money and throughout the course of their conversations, he never missed an opportunity to present quick, unsolicited details of his unprecedented luck and success at a decade-long trade in helicopters and speed boats. Despite his friend's outwardly earnest crack at transparency, Disun bore an unyielding doubt, and as unfair as his reservations seemed, he knew better than to take Ige's every word as the gospel truth. He couldn't resist the nagging feeling that his friend, out there in the U.S., had been associating with the underworld. Disun, for his part, shared his banking experience, narrating stories of his rise through the ranks within the industry, until he had now become an Executive Director in one of the major commercial banks, with a clear shot at becoming Managing Director sometime in the future.

"You have done very well, Disun," Ige said, as they left Flamingo Hotel and commenced the walk to Disun's parents' house.

"So have you, Ige. So have you. Who would have thought… who would have imagined that we'd make it this far?"

"The odds were incredibly, Disun," Ige's semi-conscious shaking-of-the-head was full of meaning.

"You can say that again!"

"Wow!"

Against Disun's protests, Ige insisted on walking him back home, and while their entourages was in tow, they kept a respectful distance, granting their bosses their well-deserved privacy. As they progressed, Disun watched Ige from the corners of his eyes. The latter's rhythmic, confident strut seemed new, fresh and while a subtle hint of his polio-gait lingered on, Ige's new stride was a far cry from the reptilian hobble that he was renown for in his youth. In some baffling way, Ige's shambling limp of the old seemed to have disappeared, and whatever remained of his old shamble appeared to have miraculously mellowed into something of a gallant, haughty swagger. Disun smiled quietly to himself. Ige would never cease to amaze him.

The following evening, they rendezvoused at one of the many alfresco restaurant-bars that were springing up in the ruins of a recently demolished district on the lagoon front. They settled for one that was well recommended by the Manager back at Flamingo Hotel, and while it seemed just as raggedy as the others from the outside, the interior was surprisingly neat and well organised. As they sat there at the table, gazing across the lagoon, the nostalgic wave was sobering.

"Just like yesterday," Disun mused, his eyes travelling deep into the distance, well across the fishermen-cluttered Lagoon, onto the glittering lights on the Island. "Just like yesterday."

"Unbelievable."

A voluptuous waitress came along and took their orders. Then she returned just as quickly, with a tray of assorted drinks balanced on her palm. There was a moment of silence, as the waitress poured their drinks. In the background, loud noises of exploding firecrackers filled the air, rattling in quick spurts, somewhat like a machine gun; and, in the distance, a pyrotechnic display of fireworks coloured the foreground, lighting the jet-black sky beyond the Lagoon.

"Can you tell the difference?" Ige ventured. "Everywhere you look, there is a constant reminder of the wide gap between those of us on this side of the Lagoon and those on the other side."

"Tell me about it. But, really, what are you referring to this time?"

"Take a look across the Lagoon. Just look at the colourful display on the other side."

"Well... We still have to give our youth some credit, though. As usual, they are putting up a great show."

"You bet they are! I mean, what's the risk of a few bloody explosions to a feisty ghetto boy?"

The ensuing laughter was spontaneous; boisterous. Obviously, they had their own memories.

"Then again," Disun said, "Standing here, from this perspective, it is difficult to tell who is who and who is on which side. Especially, given that velvety sleek Bentley packed in your reserved slot at the hotel. It's becoming increasingly difficult to tell which side you're on."

"Now, see who's talking. You actually think I am totally ignorant?" Ige chuckled. "Trust me, Olumide has filled me in on your progress on Broad Street. Corner office, big cars and all what not."

"You'd better not believe anything that that young man tells you."

"Well, I guess I still have the exclusive prerogative to my beliefs."

"Well then, what can I say?" Disun picked up is glass and took a sip. "Whatever the case, let's face it: we've done well."

"Certainly, we have. And, what a ride!"

"Well, let's give thanks."

"Always, my brother. Always."

There was silence. The excitement of the previous night had subsumed, and the realm of spontaneous chatter had worn itself out. Their thoughts are now perched on deeper curiosities, and as the silence lingered on, it seemed as though they were both contemplating their next line of conversation – the next question, perhaps – yet, they both also seemed to recognise that they were many years ahead of their youthful chummy days, and, therefore, mutually reserved a new level of respect and discretion

It helped that the DJ chose to play a musical video on the 20-inch TV just that moment. In no time, the Afro Beat rhythm emanating from the TV complemented the sound of the current licking against some nearby canoes. Suddenly, Fela sprung onto the screen, all seventy-five kilos of fire-breathing, tongue-twisting, chain-clanging genius. His half-clad torso of glistening, wiry muscles moved in perfect sync to his own supernatural tunes summoned at the behest of an unusual mind. As Fela delivered his deep rhetoric and intricately choreographed movements, Disun could visualise his polarised world as an opposing squad of angels and demons, locked in a fierce contest for his soul.

"Just look at him," Ige said, punctuating Disun's thoughts. His tone seemed to have suddenly attaining a pensive edge. "A rare essence of courage in an ocean of the meek."

"*Eleenia!* Lone sheepdog amid a million sheep; daring to look the wolves straight in the eyes. One of the few brave ones."

Seeming to have found sudden inspiration, Ige reached in the box of *Montecristo* before him and lit a cigar with fanfare. Disun didn't miss the faint, yet distinct herbal whiff beneath the cigar's smoke. Ige, apparently, had found a clandestine way to perpetrate his custom.

"Old habits die hard, eh?" Disun teased.

"You're funny," Ige said, re-igniting his cigar with studied absorption, paying sparse attention to his friend's jibe. "But I have a world of respect for people like Fela. At the end, it isn't enough for us to simply sit here, smoking expensive cigars, and celebrating our luck at escaping the ghetto. In reality, how many of our contemporaries did? How many had the chances that we had? Or, let me put it this way: how many had the courage to do what we had to do to get here?"

"Well said, Ige. I share the same burden. It's always mixed feelings every time I come around to visit my folks. On the one hand, I feel grateful to have come this far and to have the opportunity to take care of my people. I also feel a sense of satisfaction whenever I look into the little children's eyes and see the glint of inspiration and hope that I seem to now represent for them. But then again, when I look deeper, especially, when I look deeply into the eyes of the older ones among them; those who have clued-in – the secondary school kid who's parents could not afford to send to university or the unemployed twenty-something-year-old father of two – I see fear; I see despair. For them, hope had been confronted by reality. And my occasional splashing of cash does nothing to elevate their spirits."

"I hear you, Brother. But I guess, the question then is: what could we do?"

"I believe that is the pertinent question: What more can we do? I have decided recently to set up a scholarship. The goal is to find the best kids in some of the Secondary Schools around here and help them through university. But then, this is merely a second-best solution. Technically, it is even more of a short-term therapeutic remedy for our own selfish consciences. Because, really, just how many kids could one sponsor? After you'd picked your winners, what happens to the many other kids that you would have overlooked? What fate befalls the one million that you would have left behind? How could sponsoring one child to college save a generation?"

"That indeed is the challenge, my brother. Ideally, this shouldn't be anyone's call. There should be a more organic, more comprehensive scheme in place; a system of sustainable, self-reinforcing opportunities. Parents should be able to send their children to good schools. Citizens should be entitled to basic education and extensive pathways to alternative carers, regardless of their career inclinations. Children should have a fair chance to excel, not only by virtue of their intellect, but also just as much on the basis of their talent, personality or good old-fashioned hard work. Every child, person, human being is hard-wired to do one thing exceptionally well. Every child is born to excel at something. The pertinent question to ask therefore is with regards to whether or not our system is designed to help individuals find their own thing? If, indeed, they do find this thing; does our system provide enough economic oomph such that they could on the basis of this one-thing excel, build a career, a company or, even, better still, an industry? Are there enough opportunities for the ambitious to find and grow their God-given talents? Are there enough industries evolving and growing organically in this manner; absorbing and developing skilled workers en-mass. The economy should be vibrant, diverse and dynamic enough to encourage entrepreneurs and industries of all kinds to flourish. This is the core responsibility of society; specifically, this is the core duty of the government. This is not something to be left to the individual, because, really coming to think of it, how much could an individual do when there is the kind of structural anomaly that we are experiencing currently?"

"You simply nailed it, my friend. This is my fundamental grouse with our governments. They don't seem to have a clue."

"Well, that is where the real challenge lies, because, at the end, who's prerogative is it, really? I had the presence of mind to figure things out early enough in life and, luckily, so did you. But then, how many of these kids could be as crazy as we were? Indeed, how many should? The thousand books that I read were useful, obviously. Of course I kept that away from you until the last minute," Ige laughed out loud. "And thank God for music. What would I have done without Fela and Mr Bob Marley? I guess without their constant, unrelenting words of inspiration … well, who knows what I would have done."

"Hmnnnn … True words. Fela and Marley literarily saved my life."

"But, seriously, when a government has failed to create legitimate means for its citizens to succeed, with whom does the prerogative lie to find a different way? I was able to decipher quickly enough in life that the choice lay with me. I owe an obligation to myself to succeed one way or another. My crooked gait was already making it difficult to stay on the straight and narrow, in any case." Ige laughed self-consciously. "But, on a more serious note. I had the gumption to take it upon myself. I did what it was that I had to do."

"Well, you did, and guess what, so did I. Thank God for wisdom. Perhaps, more importantly, thank God for courage. But since you brought it up, Ige, we have to give credit where it is due. You have obviously done very well for yourself. I am really curious to know what your experience had been?"

"So have you, Disun. So have you. And I am just as proud of you as I suppose that you are of me. What had my experience been?" Ige took a long draw at his cigar, exhaled slowly, stared into the distance for a moment, and slowly shook his head. "Wow. What a ride. Where do I even start?"

"I guess from the last time I saw you; before you disappeared…" Disun pulled a reproaching smile.

"Hmmm … you see …" Ige paused for yet another moment. He seemed to be reflecting over his next words. "The age-long quest for achievement had always been a dialogue with your conscience; a perpetual struggle with your inner-self. You remember that conversation that we had one of those nights, sitting by the lagoon, just as we are now, talking about life, success and crossing over? Do you remember?"

"You're teasing me, of course? How does one forget an episode like that?"

"Certainly. And, if my memory serves me right, I think we probably even went as far as to have a bet."

"Well, yes. We actually did."

"Of course we did. But I guess that's beside the point now. You see, Disun, ambition is a perpetual onslaught on the purity of one's soul. I guess, from my perspectives, extra-ordinary success is not a function of how far you have come in life; nor is it of how much you have been able to accomplish. Rather, true success is a function of your residual self. I'll explain: The key question after all said and done, fundamentally, is how much of the true *you* remains? How much of your integrity, your morality, your humanity – how much have you been able to retain? The currency for worldly gains, my brother, is a share-of-your-soul. In most cases, the merchant is the devil. Lucifer. That's the real enemy on this journey – trust me – or the real friend, depending on which side of the divide you have chosen to pitch your tent. Little wonder the pilgrims aim their symolic stones at him in Mecca. *Esu laalu, ogiri oko* – our Yoruba's would say. You can notice that this coalescence of cultures transcends coincidence. Lucifer is the universal adversary."

"Well, some have said that we Yorubas descended from Nimrod… or Lamurudu. So, obviously, there could have been some interaction between the two peoples. I mean the Yorubas and the Arabs."

"So you see my point. But these aren't obvious things. The average Joe doesn't see this. Anyway, sorry for the digression." Ige choked on his cigar and coughed vigorously to clear his throat. "I guess it's my genius kicking in."

"Well, it's allowed."

"I thank you. So…it all boils down to the soul. Now, even the Bible spoke of the rich, the camel and the proverbial eye of a needle. Some people have found a direct link between the realization of worldly gains and one's propensity to expend this most-intrinsic currency. How much of this dispensable asset you are willing to trade. Some – in their cunning – even opt for the choice to mortgage; hoping to redeem before the day of reckoning. But for most, it is often too late."

A lingering silence followed. Ige held his cigar and tapped away pensively on the large cowry ashtray on the table before them. Then he looked away into the distance, allowing his gaze to linger on the dancing waves.

"I see you still love love to flex your intellectual brawn, don't you?" Disun said, hoping to end the silence.

"I take that as a complement, Disun. What else have I got? But, frankly, I am surprised that you see this merely as a mental exercise. I am trying to show you where I have been."

"I am with you, Ige."

"Let's put it this way: in the quest to succeed, there are people who have had to dine with the devil."

"Hmnnn... I hear you. "

"There are people who have been handed success, not necessarily on a platter of gold, as we both know that they wouldn't; but, rather, on a splatter of blood. There are those who have been too far mislaid."

"Now, Ige, that's deep."

"Well, how deep do you want this to get?"

Disun could feel the tension in the air. Clearly, there were certain things that Ige wanted to say; things that he wanted to reveal; but Disun could also sense that the latter was anxious; tentative; reluctant. Disun was, himself, perhaps just as nervous as his friend, because, at the end of the day, he couldn't say with certainty that he was ready for the revelations that were poised to come to life. Were these disclosures bound to change his perception of his friend forever; or affect the nature of their relationship? Or, even still, was the real impact going to be on his psyche, leading to a radical transformation of his worldview? Are Ige's revelations going to change *him*?

"Well, I left the shores of this country with Alani... the Baale's son. Of course you know who Alani is. Everybody knew Alani those days and I remember that we even went to see him together during one of his visits. Alani clearly wasn't doing badly at all. And on one of those occasions when I went to see him, I pleaded with him for a way out of the ghetto. I wanted to go with him to the States. He turned me down on a few occasions, but I guess, eventually, when he realised how serious I was, he made me an offer. It wasn't an easy decision. It was a bit unnerving at first, because his offer came with a baggage, laterally, including some rather serious obligations." Ige paused, reflected, puffed at his cigar; exhaled. "But when I thought of the alternatives, it all became easy. When it came down to it, it was a no brainer. I guess a lifetime of pain in the ghetto had prepared me for that one occasion – that one decision. My consent couldn't have been more affirmative. From then onward, I knew I had crossed the line. There was going to be no turning back. However, I was ready."

"Something tells me yours had been a more interesting experience than mine."

"You're being a smart ass now, Disun." Ige laughed a dry, ambiguous laugh. "But let's just say that these two eyes of mine had seen so much; these two hands, done so much. But I guess I'll save the details for another time and place. For now, let's just enjoy this beautiful evening, this nice view, these fine drinks and this unbelievable reunion."

Disun was disappointed that his interjection had cut his friend short, and now that the latter had retreated, he cut his loss. "Most definitely, my friend …"

Ige raise his glass in a toast. "To life."

"To life, and living — with all its pleasures and pain."

CHAPTER 23

DOREGOS LOOKED REGAL behind his large glass desk, appearing every bit a cosmopolitan monarch, as he always did and looking very much in control. He had a sweltering can of Coke set on the table and a handful of groundnuts in a small pile on the table. For someone who prided himself in his sense of detail and decorum, this small streak of sloppiness, as immaterial as it might seem, was testament to graver issues. Dorego's orderliness bordered on an obsession and any dint of tardiness was a manifestation of something deeper.

Disun came into the room and took a seat before Doregos. One quick look at his boss's face and his concerns were confirmed. The strain on Doregos' face and the colour of his eyes were unsettling. There was obviously something bothering him, but Doregos, in his usual style was doing his best to look normal.

"I hope that you have been notified of the scheduled trip to Texas this weekend for the World Oil and Gas Conference. It's the MD, me, you and a few other executives. I believe you have a valid US visa?"

"Yes I do, Sir."

"Okay then. Do prepare yourself. I thought I should bring that up, since it crossed my mind, just to confirm that you are aware and ready."

"Yes I am, Sir."

"Excellent. We'll chat later."

"Okay, Sir. But I trust you are okay. You seem a bit tired."

Doregos did not respond right away. "Well, everything is okay. By and large. Just a couple of issues coming up. I guess we'll have sufficient time to discuss in Texas. Let's leave everything till then."

"Okay Sir." Disun took his leave.

Upon their travel to Houston Texas that weekend, Disun and his boss arrived to the comforts of Four Seasons Hotel. Over the years, Disun noticed that the social gap between him and Doregos had virtually disappeared. Whenever they travelled, they both flew Business Class and unlike in the past when they would have checked into different wings upon their arrival at a hotel, they now took similar rooms, often side-by-side at the executive wing.

That Quorum's Managing Director was also in Houston and in the same hotel didn't come to Disun as a surprise. However, as he approached the buffet table at the restaurant later that evening and saw that familiar feminine profile, he felt a brutish hand grip his heart. Though she had her back turned towards him, the amplified hourglass figure was unmistakable. He knew who it was. He edged closer to the buffet, fell in line behind her and quietly, said, "Hello."

Abeni turned around, seeming just as surprised as he was. "Disun. Wow. Surprise, surprise."

"I didn't know you were on this trip."

"Neither did I."

"Very interesting …"

"I am with the MD's team. We got wind that The Chairman of First Oil – Alhaji Bashiru – was going to be here. We have been chasing his account for a while and once we learnt that he was coming for the conference, the MD felt it was a good opportunity to seek his attention."

"And you are obviously the best suited to seek this attention?" Disun winked with mischief.

"Don't be funny. It's not what you think. This is strictly business. Strictly professional. You should know from experience that these big men tend to be more attentive whenever they are out of the country. They tend to be more relaxed; more accessible. Besides, Alhaji is not like that. He is a very respectable old man."

"Well, I'll take your word for it."

She shot him a quick, menacing look. "Come on. Stop being a nuisance."

They both laughed. The next few minutes were focused on filling their plates; or, more aptly, trying not too. Afterwards, they proceeded to a table in an intimate section of the restaurant, next to the window with a charming view of the hotel's garden and swimming pool.

"So, what brought you?" Abeni said, once they were settled at the table.

"Routine, really. I attend the conference every year, so long as I can squeeze out the time."

"I suppose you're with Doregos, then?"

"Yes. Doregos is also here."

"I see. And how is the trip panning out?"

"So far, so good. Of course, we are still at the early stages. I need the conference to start so that I can establish which of the big shots are here this year. I guess it is more of a networking event for me, at the end."

"A secret vacation?"

"I am definitely not complaining."

The laughers were unprompted, frequent. The atmosphere was beginning to soften, and while his vision of the *Alien Woman* endured, Disun was beginning to recognise and enjoy a more natural, amiable side of Benny's.

"How long are you in the US for? Any holiday, plans after the conference?"

"Well … " Abeni paused, as though reflecting on something. "I plan to stay on for another week. I will be jetting off to New Jersey right after the conference."

"Hmnnn… sounds like an interesting plan. So, what's happening in new Jersey?"

"Well, nothing serious – just visiting. Family and friends, basically; nothing out of the ordinary."

Disun sensed a hint of evasiveness in her response; but, then again, he was already struggling to suppress his paranoia. "Nice."

"So, how about you?"

"Straight back to Nigeria. Some of us are not as lucky as the rest of you are. Too much work waiting back at the office."

"Indeed. As though we are completely ignorant of your antics. Isn't it common knowledge that you spend half of your time hobnobbing with the movers-and-shakers of society? Playing golf and flying around in their private jets?"

"You must be mistaking me for someone else."

"Yes indeed, I am."

"Okay. So you got me there. But you know as much as I do that the biggest deals are consummated on yachts and golf courses. I'm sure you have seen your fair share of these."

"Certainly. Well, really. When it comes down to it, what really matter are the results. Whatever gets the job done."

"Excellent. We are finally on the same page. So, I guess we're square, then. What more can I say."

They laughed out loud once again. Then, there was an extended period of silence, with each avoiding the other's eyes.

Disun raised his glass. "To many more high-flying years."

Abeni raised her glass to his and clinked. "Wish you the same, player."

Disun came into Dorego's suite, and was taken aback by his boss's appearance. It was already noon, and, somehow, Doregos was still in his pyjamas trousers, though he had chosen to wear a linen shirt over this, which, he had left partially and wrongly buttoned. He sat at the largest sofa in the living section of his suite, a pile of newspapers to his right, banking paperwork to his left and the paraphernalia of coffee on the occasional table beside him. The coffee table in the middle of the room held a half-drunk bottle of brandy, beside which a crystal glass sat half-full. The TV was on CNN, barely audible, and the radio-clock on the bedside locker in the room was churning out European football league commentary in deep Cockney. For some reason, the blinds were yet to be drawn – even though it was noon – and the entire room was engulfed in the smoke that, apparently, had been emanating from Doregos' cigars for hours. As Disun took his seat, struggling to re-calibrate his breathing, he could see the cloud of smoke clinging to the ceiling. For a moment, he felt as though he were in a burning house. Or, perhaps, he was, for in all the years that he had worked with Doregos, he had never caught the latter in such as state of disarray and unfathomable mess. In all the episodes of trials and tribulations that they had weathered together, not once had he been presented with any version of his boss bearing a remote resemblance to what was now before him. The shock that he experienced was beyond comprehension. What was going on?

Doregos offered him brandy, which he politely refused, as he always did. That had been their offer-and-refusal routine from the get go, but Doregos – being the creature of habit that he was – would always ask. Ironically, all other established habits of Doregos' seemed to be falling apart that night, if his physical appearance and the state of his suite was anything to go by; and, Disun was very worried.

"You seem a bit tired, Sir." Disun's understatement was on purpose. "I hope you're doing okay?"

"What do you want me to say, Disun? That all is well?"

"I'm just a little worried, Sir," Disun volunteered. "I haven't seen you like this in a long time." Disun, again kept his tactical understatements. The truth was that he had never seen his boss in such a state of discomfiture.

"Well, to put it mildly: all is not well."

"I am really concerned to hear that, Sir." Disun's surprise seemed exaggerated, since Doregos was merely stating the obvious. However, on a second thought, the mere fact that Doregos was openly admitting his turmoil, in itself, could be alarming.

"You do not have to be. I already saw this coming. I have been playing this game for so long, and if anything, it was clear that the game would come to an end at one time of the other."

"Would it be appropriate if I ask what is going on Sir?"

"You will know. There is really nothing to hide anymore" Doregos paused and reignited his cigar. Then after a few flowery puffs and a moment of silence that, from Disun's position, could have been a millinium, he spoke again. "I am being side lined. I am being pressured out of the Bank."

"How so, Sir? How is that possible?"

"You are still in touch with your roots, aren't you?"

"Very much so, Sir."

"Then I'm sure you're familiar with the term *Ote*?"

"To a large extent, Sir."

"So, enlighten me."

"*Ote* means politics; the negative side of politics, perhaps."

"Well, you may be right. But in the starker sense, *Ote* describes a conspiracy… and when sustained for a long time, it could also describe a cold war."

"Yes Sir."

"That's the idea. Alonso Biobaku and some key people on the Board had been playing this game for a while. It had been a delicate game, because we all understand – from both sides – what this is all about. The point had always been that these people reserve a certain measure of respect for me and what I am capable of. Call it fear, if you would. I mean, who wouldn't? To the extent that I basically came from nothing and I had come this far – all by myself; singlehandedly – they always feel the need to put a leach on me."

He paused to pull on his cigar.

"They also know that the Bank could not have achieved what it had achieved without someone like me in the system. In actual fact, if we are to be brutally honest, they know that the Bank may have ceased to exist without me. They know what they have asked me to do for them in the past and what they are still asking of me as we speak. But at the same time, they hadn't seem to be able to rid themselves of some inherent paranoia that they have – I mean, I didn't attend their Ivy League schools, for instance, neither am I from their fancy backgrounds; nor am I married to one of their sisters or first cousins. Yet, I have, one way or another, made Quorum what it is today. They could argue back and forth and attempt to discount my contributions – which they have the habit of doing from time to time – but we all know what the truth is. They all know what I have done for the Bank over the years. And to the extent that the secrete of the their success is literally in my hands, I have them by the balls, and, by extension, I have the Bank by the balls. This concerns them, as it would anyone. And. In spite of all their assurances, they often play it out in their decisions."

Disun nodded and made intermittent listening sounds.

"You may be aware that Alonso's tenure expires in six months?"

"Well, I got wind of this, but somehow felt it is still further ahead…"

"No. It's actually in six months … and ordinarily, who should be next in line for the MD-ship?"

"Your good self, Sir."

"*Abi?* It should be a no-brainer, shouldn't it?

"Certainly, Sir."

"Well, I am sorry to disappoint you, but it isn't? Nothing is that straightforward with these guys."

Disun stuck to his listening noises.

"They want me out. They want me out perhaps because they think they will not be able to control me. They cannot predict where I play. And, I cannot blame them, could I? They could be a little laid back, but they are not exactly as dim as one might think. Even when I always have my hands folded behind me when I speak to them, and my sentences are punctuated with a thousand "Sirs", they are still smart enough to see the contempt and absolute disregard that I have for them. Not for all of them, though, but, specifically, this conniving clique that I am talking about. Unlike them, I am a self-made man. I have no Godfathers that they could approach to appease me – should I somehow fall out of line. We have no mutual uncles that could mediate outside the Bank. No mutual fathers-in-law. I am a lone wolf. An outlier. A non-respecter of men; let alone lesser men. Who wouldn't be afraid of someone like me?"

Disun continued to listen with his eyes. It was as though he were floating.

"So, finally, in submission to their perpetual state of cowardice, what have they decided to do? They have shown their cards. They have decided to cook up a scandal. Imagine these ungrateful clowns. They are cooking up a huge scandal against me. They even have the effrontery to base this scandal on an errand that I once diligently ran for them." Doregos shook his head in an exaggerated gesture of resentment. "There is a lot of filth going on as we speak. *Rikisi, Arekereke, tembelekun.* Even some officers who are supposed to be loyal to me have jumped on the bandwagon. They still smile every time they come into my office and still go around saying their phoney 'yes-sirs' all over the place. They think I am ignorant of their involvement; their ploy. They would all eventually know what they are playing with. Perhaps, the most important lesson you are going to learn from me tonight is that you should never trust anybody one hundred percent. Not me; not even your father from whose loins you were conceived. Everybody has an agenda, with a role clearly spelt out for you. All would be dandy, until you deviate from your role; or, as the case may be, until you lose the capability to play that role. That is when you see the true colour of men."

"This is really unfortunate, Sir."

"Well, it depends on whose perspective you are seeing it from. From my perspective, it is okay. I have been expecting this for a while, and as bad as it may seem, it actually turns out to be a huge relief. For them on the other hand, I doubt if they realise what they have gotten themselves into. *Yiyo ekun*, my young friend, *bi ti t'ojo ko kee. Haba!* Even you should know that!"

Disun had never heard Doregos speak so many words in vernacular in such quick succession. The reality is that he could possibly have never heard him speak that many Yoruba words altogether. Doregos was veering off all of his usual protocols. Whatever it was that was going on in his mind and in his life could not have been more disrupting.

"I am feeling you, Sir."

"You haven't even started feeling me yet. You just be patient. All I am awaiting is for them to come into the open with their ploy; then I will hit them. I will hit them so hard; they would have neither the time nor the willpower to react. You should know that I am serious when I said that I have their balls in my hands."

"I believed you, Sir."

"You had better do, because as you are sitting here right now, you have a very key role to play. The important point to note is that I and, indeed, we, have to profit from this intrigues. We have to turn this shenanigan in our favour. For one, I am taking a few of these guys down with me. That is as certain as nightfall – except I am not the true son of my father. However, it is not sufficient to only disgrace and destabilize these guys. It is also important to profit from their machinations. Since they have conspired to rob me of a future at Quorum; I have taken it upon myself to create a retirement plan."

"I'm with you, Sir." Disun's attentiveness was turned up a notch.

"You had better be." Doregos took an extended drag at his cigar and once he had exhaled most of the fumes into the saturated atmosphere, poured himself a drink and downed it in one swift gulp. "Now, here is the plan…"

Doregos proceeded to lay down his plans: Ever since the Central Bank announced its banking industry capitalisation and consolidation effort a few months earlier – insisting that all banks raised their minimum share capital from four to twenty billion naira, and aiming in the process to trigger a wave of mergers and acquisition deals among the banks to consolidate the industry from its current ninety small, feeble and undercapitalised banks to twenty – the mad rush amongst the banks to meet the recapitalisation deadline had been intense. Once the Central Bank Governor had made it clear that any bank that failed to meet the deadline would be taken over by the Apex Bank and forcefully assigned to a bigger bank under a forced acquisition arrangement – and being that the CBN Governor had not earned his reputation by issuing idle threats – the majority of the banks had summarily shifted the bulk of their strategic and operational capacity towards the realisation of their capitalisation goals.

Quorum, just like all the other banks, was neck deep in the wave of strategic, operational and Public Relations activities that would help to bring about success at their recapitalisation quest. The whole industry was agog with activities. Consultants were hired. Budgets were set aside and the Nigerian banking industry resembled a pumped-up triathlon, with the sole aim of every competitor not necessarily to win, but to survive. Like raptors seduced by the whiff of a sea of carrion, the world's top Mergers and Acquisitions consultancies flew in their brightest stars in torrents, each mapping out a semi-secret reconnaissance missions, hoping on the prospects of an opportunistic gain. Yet, their local rivals stood their ground, bracing up for a fierce contest, when, eventually, the bidding wars commenced.

"Quorum had been working on a grand scheme," Doregos volunteered. "And, all along, not only had I been the architect, but, I had also been the chief executor." Doregos continued.

According to him, Quorum's official plan for a successful recapitalisation had been two-pronged: the first prong involved the mobilisation of funds through Private Placement Schemes, by soliciting large investments from strategic investors, often wealthy individuals, corporate interests and private equity managers. If things worked out according to plan, Quorum would have generated a third of its recapitalisation funds this way. The second prong of this plan involved the mobilisation of massive funds through an Initial Public Offering of its shares on the Nigerian Stock Exchange. In the preceding weeks, Quorum had employed a collage of big-name professional companies to provide it with the additional energy that it deemed necessary to propel it to its re-capitalised future as seamlessly as possible. With a seemingly limitless budget, these companies had gone to work with gusto.

"But all that rhetoric on the two-pronged plan as well as the flurry and fiesta accompanying it, like everything else that goes on in the Bank, is a charade. I mean, to a large extent, the Private Placement and the IPO will go on as planned, but that is as far as that goes. Everything else is a show. As you may have learnt by now, there are two versions to everything that goes on behind the big corner office doors at Quorum. Some, such as the Private Placement and IPO are fit for public consumption. Some aren't. So, to the extent that you are now a player, I will share some of the more – should I say discrete – versions with you. Now, here is what Quorum is not saying:"

As Doregos was to reveal, the bank, relying on the resourcefulness of an elite team of super highflyers – led by none but Doregos himself – had come up with a parallel plan to orchestrate the capitalisation process and, thereby, retaining ownership and control of the Bank. The first aspect of this plan involved the utilisation of large tenured deposits placed by a select group of high-volume customers' to buy and consolidate substantial shares of the bank during the Private Placement exercise, warehousing these under a series of quickly-established shell companies. These shares were to be appropriated at a future date among the chief players in the scheme, including the bank's leadership and some of the directors. Should any of the depositors call to liquidate their deposits during this "operational" period, the bank, being a bank, and counting on the fundamental knowledge that such an event could only, ordinarily, occur in isolation, would always be in the position to accede. However, at he end of this exercise, once the trading suspension is lifted, the bank would take out a week or two for the last leg of the process, that is the pay-off.

Under the pretext of an extended post-IPO computation and administration period, the bank would delay its announcement of the results, which, essentially, entails a summary of the total number of shares issued and over-subscription details. While subscribers await this announcement, the Bank's shares would have started trading on the Stock Exchange, and the price would have risen, as again most subscribers' shares would still have been locked in the induced bureaucracy, preventing them from reaching the market, thereby driving artificial scarcity. By the time the Bank announces the over-subscription details including how many shares they would be issuing and how much of the subscribers' pledged monies they would be returning due to over-subscription, they would have realised enough value appreciation on their existing shares – from their old shares and private placements – to pay for their newly assigned acquisitions while at the same time paying off the oversubscription. Quorum would even aim to garnered enough surpluses during these few weeks of flux to invest in short-term money instruments yielding extra-ordinary returns towards their equity expansion plans.

The second parallel plan involved the issuance of phantom loans to a cartel of *known* customers – with the word *known* primarily qualifying the bank's knowledge of these customers' disposition towards graft. Broadly, these companies were being solicited to take fictitious loans, based on blown-up funding requirements and secured with assets carrying inflated market values. These loans would be hurried through the approval process and upon disbursement, most of the proceeds would be harvested and deployed in mopping-up the Bank's shares from the market; the remaining would be utilised to cover transaction costs and to pay the collaborators a "service charge". Naturally, many of these loans would eventually go bad, and at the appointed time, the pledged assets would be realised at a third of the documented value. The loans would be moved into a recovery portfolio and a bunch of naive Bank employees would be assigned to go-after the debtors. Of course when the statutory period eventually elapsed, the loans would be provisioned for, written off and taken off the Bank's books. The only victims in the end would be the fall-guys, who, having been pressured into booking the loan in the first place, would be summarily dismissed or asked to resign; they along with the crop of legitimate, trusting shareholders who would remain oblivious to the nascent scam that had secretly skimmed huge percentages off their shareholding ratios.

"I – singlehandedly – am the chief architect and chief executor of this scheme." Doregos bragged, getting on his feet and beating his chest like an aroused silverback. "Which, amongst those imbeciles has the brains … which amongst them has the heart. It takes a lion's heart to do these sorts of things. This is not a small boy's game."

Doregos returned to his sit and poured himself a drink.

"I hear you, Sir, " Disun said, perhaps reasoning that some sort of feedback was due at that point; yet lost as to what exactly was appropriate for him to say.

"Yes. It is I, Adigun, that God has used to sort them out. And, depending on how you may want to look at it, you could even say that it was the Devil that used me. Whatever the case may be, they had a foolproof plan for reaching their capitalisation goals without ceding control. If anything, they would further consolidated their control of the Bank." Doregos paused and shook his head pensively. "Yet, it is this same me that they have chosen to make the sacrificial lamb. Imagine!"

Though again dismayed by Doregos' revelations, Disun reaction was disproportionate. "How is that possible, Sir? They must have completely lost their minds." He was barely an inch from falling off the edge of his chair.

"You better believe what I am telling you. I guess these wimps believe I am getting too powerful for their liking. I mean, they'd always known that though. But I think they've finally mustered the courage to act."

"But how, Sir? How could anyone imagine that they could remove you from Quorum?"

"Well, so I thought. But really, if I were to be honest, I had always known that this day would come. I knew that they would eventually try. But, as I believe you probably already know, I am not one to fold my arms and watch. If that's their plan, let them bring it on. They will see fight like they had never before witnessed. They would see war!"

"But, Sir, what is their angle, really? Where are they coming from?"

"I believe that they are working with some highly-placed regulatory officers. The same schemes that I designed and deployed to safeguard their interests, they now want to use against me. Of course they are claiming that they knew nothing about it; that the Apex Bank's auditors found things out by themselves. Yes, we all know that is true, since we were all born yesterday. So, they are playing this game and I am watching, and playing along with them. But then, what they haven't realised is that I hold all the aces. For one, I have acted on very clear instructions with regards to everything that I had done and, unbeknown to them, I have them on record. Whether it's an email, or a signed little note, even telephone conversations recorded on my cellular phone, I have everything on record. They really think I am stupid, but then, that is their great undoing. This is how I am going to bring them all down with me. But for now, as far as they are concerned, I am the victim, and they are all having a field's day.

"Secondly, I did not entirely follow their instructions with regards to the shell companies. For each of the fifteen shell companies that we registered, I registered another company with a similar name – a very similar name. For every Stingray Nigeria Limited, I registered Stringray Nigeria Limited. Of course, Stingray was registered to trusted proxies – I'm not as stupid as some of these guys would be happy to think – but the real Jocker is that the clandestine funds were routed through my own Stringray Limited, rather than theirs, and you wouldn't have to be a rocket scientist to be able to guess in which company's name the targeted shares were registered. Would you be surprised, therefore, if I announced to you, that one way or another, I have – using this approach – cornered eighty percent of the entire new portfolio of shareholding that was created this way. I had of course presented them with phoney paperwork all along. I had always had my suspicions about these guys, and I had never let my guards down. At some point when I was doing all these, some faculty in my mind was saying that I was just being paranoid; that I was going too far. But judging by how things are now playing out, thank God I was!"

"What can I say, Sir. This has been such a revelation."

"Well, I am not done yet. There's more… and this is where it really concerns you."

For the umpteenth time during the course of the night, Disun was taken aback. Just when he thought he had heard it all, Doregos hit him with the bumper. This time, he had no mechanism for managing his reaction

"Really, Sir. Anything I need to do, Sir. I needn't explain how deeply entrenched in your camp I am."

"Well, I'm hoping that I already know that. And, I am hoping that I am correct, because, as you are just about to discover, you have a huge role in the next phase of my plan." Doregos sucked hard on his cigar, and rolled out a huge cloud of smoke. "Trust me, my brother, this next sequence of events will usher in a new order of things at Quorum."

"I'm with you, Sir."

"What I am saying to you, basically, is that, believe it or not, you are going to be the next Managing Director of Quorum Bank."

Disun almost fell off his seat from the impact of Doregos' bombshell, "You're pulling my legs, Sir."

"Certainly. Since I shared the same joke with you yesterday," Dorego's sarcasm was borne out of impatience.

"I apologise, Sir. I was just completely surprised by your statement." Disun could hear the pounding of his heart. He had to thread carefully. "I just couldn't believe what I was hearing."

"You'd better believe it, young man. I – Olajide Adigun Doregos – will singlehandedly crown you as the Managing Directors of Quorum – Except I am not the true son of my father. Then, once the deed is done, I will be watching over you as the Chairman of the Bank – *De facto* or otherwise."

"Wow. I am completely speechless, Sir. What have I done to deserve this?"

"It is more like, what have those bastards done? They are the ones who have created the right conditions for this takeover. And since they have ensured that I could not reach the pinnacle, I, also, in the same token would ensure that none of them did. It's going to be a stalemate; but luckily, at the end, I hold the ace. Now, given that as it may, who best to handover the mantle of leadership to? Disun, you have been a loyal protégé; a true ally."

" I appreciate your trust, Sir. I am very grateful; and I will never let you down."

"Well, that much I believe." Doregos leaned forward. "Now, here's what we need to do."

CHAPTER 24

FOUR SEASONS HOTEL WAS THE EPITOME of five-star luxury, offering a collection of exotic restaurants, three distinctively themed bars, extra-large banquet halls, a surfeit of plush lobbies and lounges; and, to top it all, extensive recreational and well-being facilities including several exotic saunas and spas. Disun had taken full advantage of the famed Four Season hospitality, spending most of the week immersing himself in the sheer abundance of luxury.

This evening, as he stepped out of his room into the generous hallway connecting the elevators, he had a different agenda on his mind. A quick glance at one of the large ornate mirrors on the velvety hallway walls gave him all the reassurance that he needed. He was at his very best. His Valentino tuxedo was sharp, clean. He allowed himself to snigger a little, remembering how long it took him to figure out the subtle nuances that differentiated a tuxedo from a suit and, perhaps, more importantly, how long it took him to accept that it was necessary to differentiate them in the first place. Having acquired a small collection of designer tuxedos of his own, he now imagined himself as some sort of expert on these nuances, and as he dressed up that night, he aimed to apply this newly acquired expertise to the utmost – not in the least because he was particularly keen to impress.

His crisp white shirt was an Armani, but his dainty black tie also reeked of Valentino's craftsmanship. Earlier in the evening, he had struggled a little in selecting the right shoes to go with his evening wear, but, eventually, he had settled for a pair of black Gucci patents, with complementary suspenders, and, that evening, for the first time, he had donned his brand-new silver Rolex – an expensive gift, courtesy of one of his billionaire clients. As he rode down the elevator, he felt accomplished; and as images of his last dialogue with Doregos flashed through his mind, he had a strong inkling of even greater things to come. These episodes gave him a unique feeling of confidence, accompanied by a reasonable measure of fear. Who would have thought confidence and fear went together? It was these same sensations that he always had, just before a major, life-changing transformation.

As he emerged at the first floor lobby, he shook the complex thoughts off his mind. He would rather be interested in keeping things simple, if only for this night. Tonight, he was out specifically to enjoy himself. The sudden barrage of flamboyant banquet-going crowd that greeted him as he turned the corner towards the huge hall where the closing dinner for the conference was being held helped him to push the infringing thoughts of the future into the remotest corners of his mind. For once, he was eager to set all strategic permutations aside, and, very simply, enjoy the moment.

As he approached the hall, he was greeted by many known faces – a few colleagues from the bank; some acquaintances he had made during his stay at the hotel; and, finally, some of the more accommodating hotel staff – then, as he entered the hall, everything exploded. The enormous chandeliers hanging from the ceiling, the gold-trimmed walls – the electric jazz filtering into the room and the joyful crowd. It was an eclectic spectacle and Disun was soaking it all in, pixel by shinning pixel. As he scanned the room for the best position to settle in, he simulteneously studied the gathering. It was a beautiful crowd, and everyone seemed to be having a great time. Everyone, including Doregos and Alonso Biobaku – it seemed – as they stood together in a corner close to the stage, half-glass in hand, laughing away and backslapping. Disun shook his head in awe, wondering at the sort of nerves that held these men together. Nothing was ever as it seemed.

He found a small group of petroleum industry executives that he knew from Nigeria and joined in on their conversation. And, just about then, dinner was announced and they all proceeded to one of the buffet lines. There was a second buffet line across the hall, and as Disun scrutinized the line for recognizable faces, his eyes came upon that familiar silhouette. By some coincidence, she also appeared to be looking around and, it was only a matter of minutes before they made eye contact. They both smiled, and, somehow, he thought he saw a furtive wink. From then on, he lost full control of his thoughts and, simultaneously, his state of mind.

He was pleased when dinner was finally over and, when he saw her chatting with one of the executives from Quorum, he saw his opportunity and moved in.

"Hello," he said. "Trust you're enjoying the evening."

"Hi." Abeni's tone was high, excited. "Sure I am. You?"

"Well, so far, so good."

The Quorum executive was gone in no time.

"It seems we are on the last lap of the banquette." Abeni said.

"Clearly. That's the closing remark, right there. You want to wait to mingle a little or would you like to take a walk?"

"A walk may be appropriate. I have had my fair share of networking with this crowd. Been stuck with them for far too long."

Disun chuckled, "You bet. OK then. Shall we?"

They navigated to the back of the hall and made their exit under the cover of the background shadows. Once outside on the hotel's sprawling grounds, they relaxed. The weather was superb: a cool breeze carried through the desert evening, ruffling the flowers and palm fronds, and the atmosphere was lit up by a full creamy moon.

The duo fell into step; taking slow, leisurely strides; and for the first few paces, they were mostly silent, seeming in unison, and sufficient in their enjoyment of the abundance of the natural beauty around them. Then, finally, they settled at a table on the pool deck and, after ordering some beverage, the conversation gained momentum.

"Benny. To be honest, I am somewhat quite fascinated by you."

"Fascinated? Hmnnn… Thant's a rather interesting choice of word. What do you mean by 'fascinated'?"

"Well, there's just something really unique about you."

"Yeah, isn't that what you all say?" Abeni's rolling-of-the-eyes was desperately overt.

"Oh no," Disun's reaction was spontaneous; almost urgent. "I wasn't referring to your uniqueness in that respect." He paused, smiled sheepishly and taking a quick sip at his soda in a frantic attempt at self-redemption. "But, please don't get me wrong, you are no doubt unique in that respect, but that isn't what I was alluding to this instance."

"Which respect?" Her face bore traces of trained mischievousness.

"Well, I guess we both know what we are talking about," Disun smiled a sly smile. "To say the truth, you are unique in more than one way. However, what I am referring to at this particular moment has more to do with your person than anything else. Your personality, perhaps."

"I see. Could you expatiate on that? "

"You see, when I look at you, I see this breathtakingly beautiful, sophisticated woman of the world. Articulate, intelligent, confident. These are the things that I see; and these – I believe – are the same qualities that everyone else sees. These are the qualities that endear you to people; scare the hell out of some others ..."

"Really? I actually scare people? That's news to me." Abeni pulled a droll facial expression reminiscent of her innocent years.

"Well, so, now you know. But, underneath this outward veneer, is another, should-I-say subtler layer of qualities, involving another set of traits and attributes, which, to me, are the most authentic, and, thereby, a more fundamental representation of whom you really are."

"Really! Are you a psychologist; or an astrologist? You surprise me. Tell me more. Tell me what I do not know about myself." Abeni rocked with studied, nervous laughter.

"Again, don't get me wrong, Benny. I am not in any way berating any of your qualities. All attributes of yours are worthy. After all, they all come together in some sort of tapestry to formulate this amazing woman that you really are. The key, however, is that some of these attributes are deeper and more fundamental to your person than others, and these are the ones that the unwary, casual observer may not notice."

"I'm amused and I'm intrigued. So, which are you, then? The non-casual observer? You could have a PhD on this topic with all the gravitas that you exhibit."

"Well, for all the time and intellect that I have devoted to this observation, I may well be worthy of a PhD. But, jokes apart, I have been observing you for quite a while. At first, all I see is this vibrant, high-flying cosmopolitan lady of the world; but then again, when I blink, and then take a closer look, I see something else entirely. To be precise, I see *someone* else entirely. I see someone from a more humble beginning. Someone from a more natural background. I see someone who has been somewhere where I had also been. Whenever I look at you – and I mean properly – I quite simply see a feminine version of me."

"Hmnn … now, you really fascinate me. I mean, you really fascinate me with all this heavy stuff. I thought we were just going out for a leisurely walk and a *tête-à-tête*; but you've come at me from a completely different angle; a totally unexpected angle. Okay, what are you getting at Disun? For one, I realise that you're trying really hard to validate a certain perception that you have developed one way or another about me. Then again, I sense that there could be more."

"I believe I am right, Benny. This applies either way. We all have our facades – we all have an outward image that we project. But underneath this veneer is our integral core, which is something that we do our best to insulate and protect from the scrutiny of the world. The reality is that this integral core shines though from time to time, and, to an attentive observer, it could be captivating. I see these things about you, Benny, and I am captivated. I sense we are similar in more than one ways. If you would permit me, I am keen to know more about who you *truly* are. Where you are from; where you have been? Where you're going. If it interests you, I am willing to share my own story with you as well. This is something that I rarely do; but then again, fair is fair. If I am going to be prying into yours, I might as well be willing to reveal mine."

Disun was stopped in his tracks by Abeni's authoritative palm. "Stop. You are talking too much."

Disun kept quiet. He could have been transposed back to the presence of his primary school headmistress. "I'm listening."

"Surprisingly – and this is really a confession – I am just as curious about you as you are about me. So, what if we make a deal. "

"OK?"

"You go first."

"How do you mean?"

"You tell me all about you, and then, I will, all about me."

"Noo, Benny. That wasn't the deal. That's not fair."

"Well, life's not fair."

"OK then. If that's what you prefer, we have a deal. Let me start by saying, very starkly, that I am from a very humble background... " Disun started to tell intimate tales about his Makoko roots, growing up with Ige and the rest of the neighbourhood kids and learning on the streets of Makoko how to aspire, innovate, hold your own and, literarily, survive. He went on to describe his first experience stepping unto the boulevards of Broad Street, how he was inspired beyond his wildest imagination; and how, through perspiration, perseverance and resolve, he had inched his way up the economic and social ladder, one tricky step after the other, until he was now where he was, at the very brink of the pinnacle. Disun was surprised by his sheer honesty as he laid everything bare, and try as he might, he was unable to determine which was the motivation for his candour: the intoxicating atmosphere as presented by the moonlit night, fresh cool desert breeze and intricate jazz from the hotels' garden speakers; or the intermittent smiles and encouragement from Abeni coupled with her expert dashing-of-the-eyes. Either way, by the time he was done, he felt naked, vulnerable and, for once, he thought he had allowed his emotions to get the best of him. In the spur of the moment, it seemed, he might have left too little unsaid.

Abeni remained quiet for a moment too long. Disun's first instinct was to get up, get away from her as quickly as possible and hide underneath his duvet. That way, he could let his rampaging emotions wear out, and hope that, with some effort, he could recover from his indiscretion. Perhaps he had misjudged her. Perhaps his revelations had been too heavy; too unlike anything that she was familiar with – anything that she knew. Perhaps he had said too much and, thereby, succeeded in unsettling her. Perhaps all he had succeeded in doing was to alienate her. Yes indeed, he had gone too far this time. He searched Abeni's face for insight into the permutations going on in her mind. He sought to find the faintest hint of her thoughts. What could be going through her mind that very moment? Was it fear; pity; or disdain? Or was she so in tune with his story that she felt empathy, or, even still, solidarity? He had no way of telling.

For a moment that counted in his mind like a year, her face remained blank. But then, just as he cleared his throat, aiming to depart under the guise of using the conveniences, and, in so doing, buy precious time to determine whether to take flight, or return to the table and fight – fight for his dignity – he saw the glistening of moisture in her eyes, and then, as he wondered if he were none other than a lost nomad in a desert pondering over the fleeting glimpse of a mirage, he saw the tumbling of a tear – he could have seen it in slow motion: the welling in her eyes, the pooling of a droplet, and the tumbling down. He could hear a sound track in the background as he dipped his hand in his tuxedo pocket and presented her with a handkerchief.

This was a more-welcome reaction.

"I'm so sorry," he said. "This was not my intention."

"Pardon me." She took the handkerchief and dabbed her eyes. "It wasn't your fault. Something just touched home."

Disun could feel the moistening of his own eyes. Benny was human, after all. She was accessible. What a relief! Gratified, he leaned across the table, reached out and held both of her hands. But then, in a fit of retrospective caution, he spun his overtly affectionate reaction into one of solidarity and care. "It's alright, Benny. I really do understand. Now, it's your turn to tell me yours."

It was a very bright morning. A few errant crickets, shrieking still; some dutiful cocks crowed with vehemence; prey and predator working together in a musical orchestra – co-performers in this inadvertent early-morning band. In the midst of this ballad, a young girl struggled to come to terms with the magnitude of her predicament. As she contemplated the sheer scale of her problems, she wished, in spite of the natural melody surrounding her, that this morning had never come.

For one, her mother would kill her. There was no question in her mind about that. At the peak of her mother's incessant burst of anger, she had seen the older woman's pupils dilate with the pure intent to kill, and while her mother's subsequent violence had confirmed her intent, the latter's knowledge of the inevitable consequences of her intended folly had reined her in. And while her mother had been inhibited by this social consciousness, she had nonetheless – on more than one occasion – been poised right at the brink of following through.

Abeni was however wise enough to know, that with the position in which she had currently put herself – and, should this reality come into her mother's reckoning – she would have inevitably robbed the latter of the last iota of scruples against committing her latent act of filicide. And now that she had an excuse – right or wrong – she would have sufficient justification to risk a potentially adverse backlash. Abeni knew that if this were the last thing that her mother did, she would follow though this time. She would have the opportunity to enjoy that unique, albeit perverse satisfaction, which, for many years, had eluded her – the perverse satisfaction of taking her own daughter's life.

"You ungrateful little disgrace of a child!" Mama Abeni would often swear. "I brought you into this world. And if I have to, I would have no qualms about sending you back. And you had better believe me when I say that."

Abeni believed her mother, through-and-through, and while she revelled in their cat-and-mouse intrigues, she had always learnt to stay within her limits. She had known not to rattle her mother beyond restraint; not to provide her with the final excuse. But throughout her twenty years of pursuing this delicate balancing game, she had also harboured a persistent fear of unintentionally crossing the danger line. After all, she was only human, and even she knew that it would only take one careless act on her part to provide her mother with the perfect excuse. *That moment had come.* That reality was here, and as she rose from her bed, fetched her chewing stick and made her way to the back of the house to commence her sanitary rituals, she knew that she was threading on an infinitesimally thin line. The situation was a ticking time bomb and it was only moments before her mother found out; and once she did, all hell would break loose.

As she made her way past her mother's room, the latter's ground-shaking snore brought her some much needed reprive; knowing that she would remain safe, at least for another hour or so while the mother travelled far-and-wide in slumber-land, or lazed around in bed, half-awake. The mother was tiring out, but this was a double-edged sword. What Mama Abeni now lacked in agility and wit, she had rather ingeniously compensated for with ferocity, cunning and – ever so frequently – sheer violence. Abeni was intelligent enough to observe this progression over the years, and, more importatntly, to register the full transformation. Her mother was now more dangerous than she had ever been.

Abeni begun to clean her teeth with the chewing stick, at first gently, and then, rather rigorously, but as she reached towards the back of her tongue and scrubbed, her stomach contracted, she gagged and, spontaneously, vomited her previous night's dinner across the earthen gutter. As she stooped over and grabbed her stomach, her body contorted over and over again, and with each spasm came the spewing of whatever remained in her rippling stomach. Finally, she was spent, and, exhausted by the spasms, she found her way back to her mat, hoping to steal a few minutes of calm to regain her strength.

Then she fell asleep.

She was awoken by the sudden, splash of a tsunami.

Then she realised that she had fallen asleep, and then realised, subsequently, and, with gratification, that she was in the middle of a dream – a nightmare – and she was going to wake up any minute. In her dream, she saw the looming image of a large woman, resembling her mother, and she yelled out her mother's name, stretching out her hands to be rescued. Then, the brutal impact of the iron bucket on her knuckle brought her back to reckoning. Her mother was standing there, quite all right, empty bucket in hand, barely reining her innermost demons in. And, as she awoke, Abeni was surprised that, at first, she was neither in dreamland, nor in a tsunami, and secondly that she was actually reaching out to her mother at her time of need. Wasn't life such a cold bucket of ironies?

Abeni scampered away from the mat, gathering her now-wet wrapper – which invariably converted into her overnight blanket every night – and attempted a dash for the door. She had to clean up the vomit before her mother saw it. She had to make the mess disappear as quickly as possible.

But then, her mother's massive frame stood like a mountain in the doorframe, blocking thoroughfare for anyone but the vermin creeping back and forth between her massive legs.

Abeni sensed grave danger. Her mother was behaving strangely.

"Where are you going?"

Of course, the mother knew where she was going. She had domestic chores to take care of. She had carried out the same chores routinely for as long as she could remember – first thing every morning before the first light of day shone through. Her mother's question was not only rhetorical, but also sarcastic. Abeni's sense of danger grew exponentially.

"Where are you going?" Mama Abeni repeated, as though she were only asking the question for the first time. "You think I haven't seen the mess in the backyard?"

Abeni felt her heart leap violently against her rib cage, and she did whatever she could to contain it. "I am not feeling well, Mama. I think I have a fever."

"Fever, *koo*, fever *niiii*. Can you not remember that not only am I a woman, but that I am also *your* mother? By default, I am wiser and more experienced than you are."

Abeni feigned befuddlement.

Her mother met her eyes and stared her down with red fiery eyeballs. "Abeni. *o ti loyun, abi?*"

Abeni's face acquired an exaggerated expression of confusion, but even as she imagined her next course of action, she prayed that the ground would open up and swallow her. "I do not understand, Ma."

"You will understand. Believe me, I will make sure that you do. Indeed, *we* would understand." Mama Abeni's voice had acquired a quiet, sinister edge. "Abeni… you are pregnant, *abi?*"

Abeni's reaction took a dramatic turn. "Pregnancy *ke? Ma'a mi*. Pregnancy *Bawo?*" She rocked with simulated impatience – a behaviour that she had never dared to exhibit in the presence of her mother. "Is pregnancy something that is contagious; or is something that leaps unto one as one walks through the streets?"

Her sarcasm was bold, brazen. Her racing mind must have reasoned that the only response to mother's imminent onslaught was for her to go on the offensive. This was a risky strategy, but she had very little to lose. She was already in a bad place.

Then, suddenly, her mother put on her own show, and the drama that followed was on a scale that even Abeni – being the chief connoisseur of her mother's dramatic bouts – had never witnessed before then.

"*Yeeeeparirpa…*" Mama Abeni let out a long, melodramatic holler. She flung her wrapper open, ran from one corner of the room to the other in her bare underskirt, landed back at the entrance, where she grabbled her wrapper, twirled it and tied it around her waist like a fat rope. Then, arms akimbo, shaking like a bass-guitarist – without the guitar – and letting out short burst of expletive between each breath, she yelled again. "*Yeepa … ori mi o …* this child has finally disgraced me. Who are you pregnant for?"

"I do not understand what you are saying, Mama. I am not pregnant let alone for anybody. I do not know how you could just wake up in the morning and come up with something like this."

The slap hit her face like the reprimand of an *Eyo* masquerade's raffia staff. Abeni escaped to the furthermost corner of the room and, in anticipation of her mother's nascent blows, curled up like an armadillo. But, uncharacteristically, Mama Abeni restrained herself. Her restraint could have come from her lack of agility or her fear of the nature and extent of Abeni's emergent defiance. Whatever it was, she stayed at the door, shouting, cursing and shaking like an exorcist.

"You are done for! This is your end, you ungrateful, useless thing. What have I not done for you? Is this how you want to reward me; with shame and ridicule before my enemies? Well, I would rather sooner kill you with my very own bare hands. Believe me – this, indeed, is your end! Except that I brought shame to those who brought me into this world. Luckily, Aunty Nurse will be around tomorrow. All I need is one test and this nonsense will be put to an end. I already know what I know, but since your mouth is still dancing like the *jobele* leaf, I will allow a neutral party to come in and give us the final verdict. Trust me, by the time Aunty nurse comes with her confirmation, that would be the end of your life. I swear by my mother's grave. Except you did not come out of this very body of mine."

For the second time that morning, Abeni found herself struggling to rein her pounding heart in. Her mother's threat was not to be taken lightly. Two things were for certain: the first being the inevitability of Aunty Nurse's routine visit to the village dispensary that Wednesday, and, inherently, her expert pregnancy tests; the second being her mother's promise of filicide, once her suspicions are confirmed.

If nothing else, Abeni knew that the affirmation of her mother's hunch was inevitable and rather than stay around to test the latter's resolve, she opted for aversion. That afternoon while her mother snored away after indulging in a surfeit of the *eba* and vegetable soup that Abeni had meticulously prepared, Abeni packed her most-valued belongings and in the evening, while her mother snored away, once again, after enjoying the beans and *garri* that, again, Abeni had meticulously prepared, she snuck out of the house, to the lorry garage, with Sisi Eko's address and a small cache of given and stolen change carefully tucked away in her bra. That night she stole away to Lagos, under the cover of darkness, incidentally in the same lorry that would ferry Aunty Nurse back to the village the following morning.

Sisi Eko was welcoming, understanding, and, in spite of the life-long feud that her benevolence towards Abeni would summarily set-off with her mother, Sisi Eko was surprisingly accommodating. Six months after her arrival at Sisi Eko's, Abeni was delivered of a bouncing baby boy named Michael, after his father, that being Sogo's Christian name. In appreciation, Sogo sent in some money to augment Sisi Eko's expenses, and beyond everyone's expectations, made a quick appearance at his little boy's naming ceremony. Subsequently, Michael became Sisi Eko's responsibility and while Abeni was away at the new school where her Aunty had enrolled her, Michael and Sisi Eko became inseparable.

Abeni was to learn a lot from Sisi Eko's independent, feminist lifestyle, and while she was not completely at tandem with her Aunt's commitment to a bachelorette life, she was quick to realize how powerful she could be as a woman, first and foremost and, then, more importantly, as a woman with the extraordinary endowments that she had been bestowed with. Under Sisi Eko's tutelage, she was quick to realise – way beyond her most liberal imaginations – how easily a woman of her stature, literarily, could succeed in the manipulation of men, weak and strong alike. The pinnacle of her learning was the realisation that with education, exposure and some rather intangible phenomenon that Sis Eko often described as "sophistication", she could deploy these feminine powers with significant reward.

Some years later when Sisi Eko got the opportunity to emigrate to England under the pretence of a tourist visa, Abeni was quick to concede the then six-year-old Michael to her care. In return, she got the liberty to pursue her education and, inherently, a clear shot at her ambition of becoming – by her definition –a very powerful woman.

"Sisi Eko had since moved to California, along with my little Michael, who, by the way is not that little anymore, since he is now fourteen. It is they that I am off to visit after the conference."

Disun was lost in amazement. This was a part of Abeni that he had never imagined. Indeed, this was a part he had never known. He was too stunned to speak.

"I assume you can understand that this is not something that I share with everyone. I'm hoping that this can remain between us."

"But, of course," Disun said, reaching once again for her hand across the table and squeezing it. "Your secrets – as I hope mine – are safe."

As he sat there under the mellow lights of Four Seasons Hotel, staring into her eyes, Disun felt a sense of self-centred relief. Abeni had her own baggage, after all. And the more they sat there in the dull light of the garden, conversing and sharing, the more something stirred in the deepest corners of his mind. It was something fresh, something unusual, yet, something that he embraced with hope and a bit of trepidation.

CHAPTER 25

THE FINANCIAL YEAR WAS DRAWING to a close and year-end activities at Quorum, as with many of the other banks were at fever pitch. Banks were working round the clock to close their accounts, while carrying on with their routine operational activities and it didn't help that the regulators had, at the same time, taken residence in their head offices and branches looking over their shoulders and breathing down their necks.

This year-end flurry of activities coincided, as usual, with the festive season, and as bankers and their consultants buried their heads in accounting books and computer records, their banking halls were overwhelmed with porters bearing complimentary gifts from satisfied and obligated customers alike, businessmen counting on a last minute, year-end windfall and upcountry-bound travellers hoping to withdraw monies for their trips. The atmosphere was usually vibrant, optimistic, and effervescent. And the promise of an extended period of celebration and holidays often added an additional hint of tension.

However, underneath this exuberance, the glittering festive decorations and the subtle humming of carols, a scandal was quietly brewing, the scope and magnitude of which was unbeknown to all but a privileged few. The absence of full knowledge notwithstanding, any observant employee of the Bank would sense that there was a whole lot more to the frenzy than the routine closing of the years accounting books. Doregos' doomsday scenario was playing out, and, finally, Disun was coming to accept that his mentor's prophecy might be coming to pass.

Two days prior, officials of the Banking Supervision Department of the Central Bank, working with their counterparts at the E.F.C.C. had swooped down on Quorum Bank's Head Office and arrested six executives, all strategic, high-ranking officials of the banks. To the casual observers' surprise, the most senior of these officials was none other than Jide Doregos. The Quorum Bank officials were detained at the E.F.C.C. Headquarters where they were faced with a laundry list of corruption and malpractices charges under the Banking And Other Financial Institutions Law. In an unusual turn of events, Doregos was granted bail on the second day, albeit under the most stringent of conditions. After news of these arrests travelled through the industry, Quorum was thrown into turmoil, and at every corner office, water dispenser, bulk-cash counting room, and drivers' lounge, people were gathered in groups of two and three, theorising about the developments, arguing quietly among themselves, and forecasting the next series of events over the coming days. A dozen versions of the contraventions leading to these arrests were in circulation. Rumours were flying around like Lagos *puff-puff* would fly off the seller's frying pan at the end of an Idumota trading day. The industry fed off this inferno like opportune raptors. Fear and panic was everywhere.

For his part, Disun did his best to fend off the avalanche of phone calls that inundated him once the news came into the open. On the surface, he feigned surprise and confusion like everybody else, but deep within him, every fibre of his being was trained on rationalising the order of events, reconciling these with Doregos' predictions and working out his own survival strategy with lightening speed. This, combined with the grinding throes of day-to-day – let alone end-of-year – operations, was harrowing.

Then, as he rode home in his Mercedes Benz that evening, the most anticipated of all the phone calls – specifically the mother of all phone calls – came through.

"Hello, Sir…"

"Disun." It was Doregos on the other side, quite all right. "You remember everything I told you?"

"Yes, I do, Sir."

"Well, I'm sure you could see the first episode as it unfolds right before your eyes."

"It is exactly as you have predicted, Sir."

"Yes. It is exactly. So, if I were you, I will be bracing up for the next stage. If I were to be entirely honest with you, only two people on the face of this earth – namely you and me – have foreknowledge of the next series of actions. I believe I could trust you to use this privilege well."

"You can count on me, Sir."

"Well, I hope I could. For your own good." Doregos laughed a dry, vague laughter; but Disun did not miss the sinister edge in his tone. "I will be checking into a discrete hotel tonight. I will call you in the morning. You must come and meet me there immediately."

"Certainly, Sir."

"Excellent." Doregos summarily hung up.

The following morning, Disun was at Dorego's hotel suite at six in the morning. He didn't leave until two in the afternoon.

They came into the conference room like the infantry – or, precisely, like officers accessing a war room. They were the Bank's elite marketing team, all looking sharp and ready. All bursting at the seams with motivation. Not unlike in the army, the men and women were all dressed in uniform, only that, in this case, rather than relying on some standard-issuance protocol, the clear uniformity in dressing was dictated by a silent dress-code – the winning dress code – handed down through word-of-mouth or by keen observation. The men were all dressed in slim fitting dark suits – black, grey and navy blue, exclusively – underneath which crisp, delicately starched white shirts peaked, forming the canvas for the more colourful designer silk ties that rested gently on them in their full, silky elegance. The men's wrists were barnacled in covert gold or silver watches; and on their breasts, the company's broche – the only standard-issued accesory– gleamed the red and violet colours of the company's brand logo. Gracing the suits' breasts pockets were flamboyant pocket squares, which, silently, conversed with the ties. The ladies' suits were even much tighter, if possible, and in place of the crisp white shirt, they donned variations of low-cut, lace-necked cotton shirts, mostly white and pastel shades, but punctuated by the occasional flashy colour. The necklaces and bracelets on the ladies' necks reeked of molten gold – 24 carats, or nothing – and the inadvertent parade of handbags on the conference table held legacies of prized, exotic animals long gone, now bearing names of legendary Italians in whose hands their costly contours had been sculptured.

The atmosphere in the room was charged, as it always was – not unlike it would have been in a war room, prior to a major offensive – and the surplus of sublime fumes from an assortment of high-end perfumes further enhanced the intoxication.

Disun walked into the room, with his characteristic gait of purpose. As he took a seat at the head of the table and proceeded to set the aim and tempo of the meeting, he assumed a serious, pseudo-military demeanour and for the first time that week, thoughts of the regulatory scandal and associated saga faded far into the background. He was a man on a mission.

Earlier in the week, word had reached him about a potentially valuable client relationship that the Bank's elite marketing team had been soliciting for a while, with minimal success, and with several previous attempts haven failed, the team had escalated their challenges to the highest echelon in the Bank's organisation – the executive management team – which, by default, was headed by the Managing Director.

However, being that Alonso Biobaku was engrossed in the on-going scandal at the bank, Disun had been asked to take leadership of the effort. Usually, Disun's role on such a marketing missions would have simply been to add gravitas and presence to the team. He would have received a quick brief just before the meeting, made an appearance with the team, go on a charm offensive with the client, and after his officers had addressed the technicalities of the client's needs, given a goodwill speech.

However on this occassion, given the crisis rocking the Bank and the resultant negative publicity, he knew that his traditional modus operandi would not be sufficient. He was saddled with the task of seducing this reluctant customer at the worst possible time, and, therefore, he knew that he had his job well cut out for him. He however approached the assignment as he always did with any difficult task: with tenacity and optimism. To give an added edge, he had summoned his most competent professionals, including the Bank's marketing mascot – which was none other than Abeni. The previous night, he had spent hours poring over the huge file binder containing every pertinent detail about the client company, it's owners and executives, its operations and the Bank's antecedence, with the intention of drawing up a foolproof strategy in wooing them over. It was during this session, sat at the giant desk at his home-office, deep into the night, that he discovered something most profound: the company's chairman, and majority shareholder was someone that he knew very well from the past; and, the Managing Director was the former's daughter, with whom he shared a closer, albeit old, friendship. He was literally thrown off his massive chair! This was beyond amazing!

White Falcon limited was part of Raptors Group of Companies – an indigenous conglomerate of seven companies with operations cutting across Shipping, Commodities, Construction and Oil-And-Gas. The company had offices, factories and logistics facilities spread across the country and at the helm of its affairs, steering this colossal operation was the father-child tag-team comprising of Chief Gbolagade Rogers as Chairman and Deroju Rogers at the Managing Director and Chief Executive Officer. Disun had always known of Raptors Group of Companies and its major operations, given that he had never lost touch with the Rogers – albeit unilaterally – and he had monitored every aspect of their social and business lives with keen interest. After so many years, and in spite of his extensive exposure over the years, the Rogers had remained one of his most reliable yardsticks for opulence. It however wasn't until he was reviewing White Falcon's file that he was able to decipher its relationship with the Raptors Group. He was vindicated when he finally learnt that White Falcon was only a recent acquisition of the Group's. With this realisation, the scheduled marketing call assumed a new dimension.

Disun found the prospects of seeing Deroju again, after so many years and such distance, overwhelming. What sort of woman would she have become? What would she look like? Was she married? Well, she couldn't have been, since she was still addressed as Deroju Rogers, going by the documentation in her company's file. But then again, women have been known to keep their maiden names after marriage; so, that in itself testified to little. He then wondered for a moment if she had children, but quickly resolved that she couldn't, since she clearly wasn't married; or was she? He couldn't even recollect what his conclusion was on that. But then again, he resolved, in this day and age, motherhood and marriage weren't necessarily correlated. Even when he may not necessarily agree with the phenomenon, he was conversant with the trend. Many of his colleagues at the Bank were single mothers. Had she kept her simplicity or had she grown to become like her mother – arrogant, class-conscious and openly condescending to the poor. He must have run a thousand scenarios through his mind before he finally decided that he had embarked on a futile mission, trying to anticipate who Deroju had become, before actually meeting her.

Deroju was as beautiful as he imagined, as gracious as he had hoped and much more down-to-earth than he would have expected at his most optimistic. The spark in her eyes upon receiving his business card was spontaneous, and they had spent the first few minutes of the meeting trying to catch up with each other, while, at the same time, struggling to stay reasonably formal and professional. It was an effort at the beginning, but, gradually, the excitement of their reunion eased, which, with some effort, and with the apparent patience and understanding of the other parties to the meeting, enabled them to bring the meeting back on track.

Once the meeting drew to an end everybody got up, exchanged pleasantries and gradually eased out of the room, leaving only Disun and Deroju, who, either by coincidence or design, managed to be the last persons to depart. They finally had their chance.

"Just look at you," Disun said, grabbing Deroju by both hands and smiling sheepishly. "What a gorgeous woman you have become."

"I am just as proud of you," Deroju said, half teasingly. "What a gentleman."

"It is amazing how much time has passed. It all seems like yesterday."

"Tell me about it."

"Well, I am so pleased to see you."

"So am I, Disun. Not in my wildest dreams would I have imagined…" Deroju paused awkwardly and Disun wasn't sure whether she was referring to their meeting, or his progress in life. "Well, I guess we would have to keep in touch."

"Certainly. Now that I have your details, I will certainly keep in touch."

"That'll be a good idea. You know where to find me."

"You can bet on that."

"I suppose you honestly imagine it's an excellent idea frolicking with this Deroju girl, don't you?" Ige's tone was casual, almost nonchalant as they sat at the alfresco restaurant on the Lagoon front of the Federal Palace Hotel pulling leisurely at the base of his cigar.

"I sincerely cannot understand your concern, Disun. What could be wrong with that?"

"While you are one of the brightest minds I know, you often seem to miss the most important points, sometimes. Just how many dozen women are out there in the world, seeking the attention of a handsome, wealthy eligible bachelor such as yourself?"

"And so what? Since when did you presume that someone like myself would be intrigued by the notion of a dozen random women looking for whatever it is that you suppose that they may be looking for?"

"What, my dear, are you then intrigued by?"

"I am past that stage now, Ige. At this particular point in my life, I am more intrigued by the prospects of a real relationship. Something genuine. Something with the potential to last."

"Could I say then that you *are* looking for love?"

"And what could be wrong with that, my friend?"

"You see? Just look at yourself. See how defensive you have become? Nobody had said that anything was wrong with that; but without anyone saying so, you already knew that by yourself– hence your defensiveness."

"I don't understand what you are saying, Ige. You are obviously in one of your hectic modes."

"The point that I am making, Disun, is that for someone as ambitious as yourself, you only have a certain pool of resources at your disposal. You are only bestowed with an infinite number of tools and, ultimately, the chances that you succeed or fail is directly linked to your astuteness at recognising and deploying these resources."

"What are you saying, Ige?"

"What I am saying to you, Disun, is that by engaging in a romantic gig with Deroju, you would be squandering one of the most valuable resources that is currently available to you."

"Now, I am completely lost."

"You aren't, Disun. Just apply yourself. Of all the uses that you could put Deroju to, a girlfriend is the best you could imagine?

"And why do you get the impression that I am – borrowing your expressions – aiming to put her to use?"

"Whether you admit it or not, that is ultimately the case. You may have convinced yourself otherwise, believing that you are going by a mutual romantic arrangement. However, at the end, you have an agenda. Period. The fact that she could be a willing partaker does not take away from a premeditated intent."

"You are hectic, Ige…"

"That however is beside the point. The key point is that engaging in romance with Deroju would be an unwise decision on your part and it would constitute an absolute waste."

"Get to the point, Ige? The more you speak, the more you confuse me. Let's leave the parables and get to the salient point."

"All that I am saying to you is that Deroju is more useful to you as a business associate – a potential ally – than a girlfriend. You can make a girlfriend out of any woman. Having an old childhood friend in Deroju's financial position is rare."

"But honestly, Ige, must every single action on your part be so cunning and calculating?"

"You had better believe that. The earlier you realise that you have embarked on a car race and you are going at a hundred miles per hour, the better. If you go to sleep, you are dead. You cannot go to sleep, Disun. You have to be awake and calculating at all times."

"Where then is the place for love?"

"Love is a mirage, my friend. Love is for the weak."

"You are truly incredible, Ige. You cannot cease to amaze me."

"But you know that I am saying the truth. You know that I am making sense. The best way to deploy Deroju is for business. If I were you, I would find romance elsewhere."

Disun shook his head in silence. He was too perplexed to speak.

Ige laughed aloud in a botched attempt to lighten the mood.

Disun remained speechless.

"It's really been exciting at the Bank these past few days, hasn't it?" Ige Said, now desperate to change the topic. Disun was grateful. He wasn't enjoying the Deroju exchange.

"Quit acting, Ige," Disun said. "You're not renown for your understatements."

Ige allowed a wide smile. "Okay then, I agree. On a more serious note, what is going on at the Bank? I am reading all kinds of stuff in the papers everyday and my feelers are providing me with conflicting details."

"Ige, since when have you become an Industry expert? And, by the way, who are these feelers of yours?"

"But by now you should know I have my ways, Disun. Information is power. Information is money. You, if not anyone else should know that. At the end, I am heavily invested in the stocks market – the banking industry, especially. And I happen to have a few solidarity shares in Quorum. I guess it's logical that I keep my ears and eyes open for happenings."

"I suppose you're right. But then, what business do you have dealing with rumour-peddlers when you could easily have found out from the source?"

"Well, Disun, if you would care to give me some credit, that, indeed, is what I am trying to do. Isn't that why we're here? It's a no-brainer, isn't it? I'd rather speak to you. But, is it not also universal knowledge that your schedule isn't as flexible as it used to be when we were kids at Makoko? Can you not remember how many times we have tried but failed to have this rendezvous?"

"Don't be ridiculous, Ige. But then again, I guess you have a point. However, you of all people can never have cause to feel that you cannot access me whenever you want to. If that ever happens, then something has gone terribly wrong."

"Okay. I hear you."

"Well, now that we are here, and having this conversation, I believe that could help set the records straight. Perhaps we should start by understanding what you already know?"

"Well, nothing concrete, really. Basically the same stuff in the newspapers. The most surprising aspect of the whole thing, of course, is the alleged complicity of Jide Doregos. I guess that should be really unsettling for you."

"Yeah, I know that would be unsettling for a lot of people. But, permit me to surprise you once again, Ige. I really am not taken aback by all this. I had prior knowledge of these events. This is a script that had been written a long time ago, and those of us who are privy to the intrigues try not to be distracted by the media fanfare."

"What exactly is going on, Disun?"

"Okay, here is the real story…"

Disun proceeded to reveal his insider knowledge and his perspectives on the happenings at Quorum Bank, starting with his meeting with Doregos at Four Seasons Hotel in Texas more than a year earlier, and culminating in a revelation of Doregos' take-over plan, including the intricate roles outlined for him.

Several moments after he was done, Ige remained silent and reflective, which was out of character for someone whose thoughts were always one step ahead of his tongue, and therefore hardly needed a reflective moment in the course of a conversation. But as Disun watched his friend this instance, he could hear his imaginative mind ticking, and not unlike a computer that had been tasked with an operational command well above it's routine, he could literally see Ige's mind spooling arduously, drawing on megabytes and battery life. Clearly, Ige was shocked by the magnitude of his revelations and was clawing and scampering for an interpretation. But then, his brainpower finally kicked in, and, Ige, being the unsung genius that he was, came to his own.

"Wow, this is heavy," Ige said, drawing hard on his cigar and letting out a dense cloud of smoke. "This is deep stuff. I think I'm going to need some assist on this one, this Cigar isn't doing it for me."

They both laughed.

Disun knew his friend like the back of his hand. He could tell when the latter was at his full form; when his gifted mind was at the verge of profundity. "Tell me. What are you thinking?"

"Hmnnnn… Disun, you may not expect what I am about to say at this very moment, but I have a very unique insight on this whole thing. I have a completely radical perspective on it."

"It doesn't take a rocket scientist to recognise that. I know you're thinking. What's on your mind? Tell me." Disun tried to veil his anticipation.

"I have never told you this, Disun, but I am sure you already know. I am a flipping mastermind – make no mistake about that; and be guided by that singular fact. I have known this for a fact since I was six years old; and, even though we never formed the habit of self-congratulation, I know that you also know. So, listen to me and listen good when I tell you that I have a completely radical perspective on this."

"I know who you are, Ige. Talk to me." Disun was going wild with anxiety, but he did all that he could to stay calm.

"This, perhaps, is going to be the most important thing that I ever said to you. So please take it very seriously."

"Tell me…"

"I see an opportunity, Disun. I see a unique opportunity." Ige said. He paused for a moment, then continued: "We've been friends for how long now?"

"Thirty-five, forty, what does it matter, Ige? We've been friends all our lives. Talk to me."

"Except I live an illusion, I could rightly say that we've been brothers. And from where I stand, I can say with absolute confidence that I have never let you down; neither you me. So, except you provide me with a reason to act otherwise, you have to trust me one hundred percent on this."

"I'm with you Ige." Disun was mentally gnawing his knuckles. "Trust has never been an issue between us."

"See, Disun, the champion mode beckons. I can see all the right signals."

Disun felt as though he had been hit by a moving train. For some strange reason, in spite of the ambiguity in Ige's statement, he attained an instant understanding. The very last statement from Ige seemed like a culmination of the many conversations that they have had over their many years of friendship. It played out in his senses like a dash at the end of a marathon. It was like crossing the finish line. Somehow, he seemed to be in mental unison with his friend and, he felt he could anticipate every word that the former was about to say. His face broke out in an inadvertent sweat.

"I am with you, Ige."

"The champion mode, beckons, Disun. And if my mind serves me well, I know it takes a special intuition to recognise it. Which is why I am unwilling to leave this to chance. I need to be sure that we are on the same page."

"I'm listening to you, Ige." On the outside, Disun strove to induce calm like the *Ikongusi;* but on the inside, he was in turmoil.

"Believe me when I say that the champion mode beacons. The champion mode is a philosophical state… a pseudo-spiritual state. It is a state of pure, unalloyed confidence. It is a sensation of floating, rising above the physical world as we know it; rising above all obstacles. It is a virtual place, and it takes a certain level of self-awareness to attain it. Occasionally in a man's life, the champion mode spreads out its arms – all that one needs to do is to recognise this preternatural spreading-of-the-arms and walk into the embrace whole-heartedly."

Disun's could not help but let his mind wander in the numinous, psychedelic world that Ige was painting before him. But he was also quick to caution himself. He had to be alert enough to consciously and coherently interpret his friend's mystic. He didn't say a word.

"Transitioning into this state comes with trauma – tantamount to a spacecraft's exertion in defying the earth's gravitational pull; or a jet breaking the sound barrier. The transitioning is often – perhaps, always – a make-or-break moment and there are neigh-sayers whose role it is to distract, delude or prevent one from this ascension. They recognise your inherent potentials and they are the quickest to see your fair chance at victory. They are often the first to see an imminent rise, even before you realise it. They also know that before this triumph comes a moment of extraordinary flux; a moment of fear and confusion; a period of unavoidable strain. As you prepare to levitate and leave all ordinary things behind. This is when their rage is at its fiercest; yet they come with subtle, quiet whispers of doubt and disillusionment. With their voiced cynicism, they try to wrestle you back to the ground, and propel themselves on the basis of your impetus. The worst among these people are those who are the closest to you. These are the people who know the workings of your innermost mind. Only they intimately know your weaknesses. When they see that you are in full recognition of who you are and even more importantly, that you know whom they are, only then would they back down. And not until then would you accede to your true calling. Then, and only then, could you ascend to your destiny. But before then, they try all that they could to manipulate and mislead you. And, perhaps, convert your momentum to their own advantage."

"I fear that you may be too calculating, Ige. Perhaps too intense."

"Really? Well, perhaps I agree. But so are you. Only that you are too consumed with reining yourself in. looking good; acting stable; conforming. This is the pattern of behaviour that is expected of a high-flying executive such as yourself. The luck that I have is that I do not have any such constraints. I do not live in that world. I never have. I never will. However, the luck that you have is that you have someone like myself on your side, as a good friend, and as an anchor. One who knows you; gets you. One with your interests in mind, and, especially, one bereft of competition or envy."

"I hear you, Ige. I do understand what you're saying. But the point is that these things are not as linear as you're putting it. And, especially, they seem to have no bearing on the issue at hand. My first instinct is to say that you've completely gone off on a tangent. But then again, knowing how your mind works, I suspect that you are building up to something."

"You're smarter than this, Ige. Focus for a minute. Apply yourself. Not all friends are bad – I mean, how could that be? After all, I am your friend, for example. The challenge comes when a supposed friend chooses to go rogue on you; when that happens, they are your worst enemies. That's all that I'm saying. Yet, a true champion would always recognise these machinations. A born champion always knows his calling. Which is why you must scheme with the cunning of a fox. And, where appropriate fight with the ferocity of a beast. You shouldn't be unwilling to fight dirty. They are most ferocious during your imminent transition into greatness. Fend them away and if they persist, go all the way."

"I mean, I get you. But at the same time, I also recognise that you are aiming to say more. Or, perhaps I am jumping the gun."

"Perhaps, you aren't. But I guess you already know where I am going with this. Ige, you have a unique opportunity. Perhaps, in all sincerity, *we* have a unique opportunity. I said 'we' because I would not have been entirely honest if I fail to declare my interest. Doregos has come up with his fancy schemes, but at the end, what exactly do you think he is trying to do? Isn't it clear that he is merely trying to use you? Utilise you as a tool to be flogged ragged and discarded when expended? Isn't it fair play, then, that you, at least, should try to spin this situation to your advantage? Shouldn't you then be the one trying to take over the Bank rather than he? I mean – I'm just saying – Doregos is in a very vulnerable place at the moment. He is a sinking man, and all that I see him trying to do is to pull himself out of the mud, using you as his human prop. Clearly, once he is out of danger, you would have to be expended. You would have to be done away with. Clearly, you would be too powerful by then; you would be holding too much information and the prospect of blackmail would always loom before him, be it real or imagined. Except there is a higher bond such as that of blood, brotherhood or a lifetime of unalloyed friendship such as the one that we have, he would never trust you. That is a dangerous recipe in any situation, let alone one involving a paranoid narcissist such as Doregos. This situation is too delicate, Disun; too volatile. It's a highly predatory world as I believe that you already know, and except you eat when you have the privilege, you will surely and eventually be eaten."

At that point, Disun realised that the time had come to come clean. "I hear you loud and clear, Ige. Don't think that I have not contemplated these sorts of things. I mean, think about it: Doregos has technically requested me to be the custodian of his loot during this period of great uncertainty at the Bank. That is a very powerful position to be in and, without doubt, a very precarious one too. So, trust me, all manner of thoughts had crossed my mind over the past few weeks. So, I had already anticipated where you were going, even before you finally came forward with the actual plan. My concern is that this may not be as simple as you have described it. Doregos could be a very dangerous man."

"But you also mentioned that he once said in the course of your deepest conversations that you should never trust anyone, including him. You should perhaps have realised that that could be the most important thing that Doregos has ever said to you; if only you were truly paying attention. Doregos is a dangerous man however you may choose to look at it, or however you may choose to deal with him. So, therefore, with you being the right-thinking guy that I have always known you to be, I hope you will agree with me that it makes good sense to, at the least, attempt to gain from this inevitably dangerous situation that you have found yourself? Disun, the attainment of extra-ordinary power and privilege always involves some kind of sacrifice. Call it compromise if you like. Someone has to lose extra-ordinarily for someone else to gain extra-ordinarily. It is a zero-some game. Which is why we do not live in an equitable world. Otherwise, wealth would be fairly, if not evenly divided among men: among nations. Those who recognise this reality earlier enough in life are those who find the advantage; take advantage – literarily – if you are inclined to see it that way."

Disun was silent for a rather long while, and Ige allowed him his moment, puffing occasionally at his cigar.

"I hear you, Ige. I mean...I hear you. However, as I continue to say, this could be dangerous. Something like this could cost us our lives."

"Well, I like the way you have just put that, because at the end of the day, we are going to be in this together. I will be with you headlong, and everyone that needs to know will know that we are a team. So, at the end of the day, my life would also be in danger. So, I am glad that you at least understood that upfront. But as I believe that you also know, I have your back. We just have to up the ante. Go the full rung. I am not an alien to violence as you may have realised. I had my fair share of turf wars and hostile takeovers. On the Streets of Chicago, my rivals were men who would have little hesitation casting a man alive in the concrete pillars of their mansions and proceed to move in with their family the following month; these are men who shipped out drugs, two ounces at a time, attached to hundreds of migratory sensor-bearing birds; men who's sophisticated drug-ferrying submarines were designed and built by some of the brightest marine engineers in the world; men who's improvised vaults were busting at the seems with cash, gold and precious stones. These are men who could put a contract on an opponent's life with a one-minutes phone call; men who believed in the core of their hearts that every product, service, skill, conscience could be bought. But, guess what, they met their match. Even they, at the peak of their arrogance, knew this. By His leave, I survived them all. Even as I am here, they are still waging wars against me, but as it was in the past, it is I who will vanquish them. Whatever the case may be, as a champion, you must choose a platform. Sometimes, you choose a platform and sometimes, a platform chooses you. I could have been a nuclear scientist, for all I care. I would have been a damned good rocket-scientist, for that matter. God knows that I am not in want of the basic prerequisites. But I didn't choose to have been born in this strange society. How do you become a nuclear-scientist in a society where men have neither the curiosity, nor the desire to explore the possibilities presented to them on earth, let alone in outer space? We were born into a society of unambitious men. So, in the absence of a legitimate platform on which to express my God-given talents, an alternative found me. Or, I found an alternative as you may be inclined to look at it. The key point is that whatever platform you choose, you may not succeed in a philosophical vacuum. As for me, I already know where I stand. I believe I make no pretences about this."

There was even more silence. Then, finally, Disun spoke: "So, for the sake of clarity, let's even say we want to pursue such an opportunity as the one now before us…what are the likely scenarios. What do we need to bring to the table, individually and collectively?"

For the first time that evening, Ige lay his cigar gingerly in the crystal ashtray beside him, leaned across the table and took his friend's hand in a firm handshake. "Now you're talking like the man that I have always known you to be. Now, I will tell you what I think."

Ige's plan involved a number of interwoven, stepwise actions that they both had to take individually and collectively over the coming weeks at the end of which they would have inevitably come into the ownership of the controlling shares of Quorum Bank. Firstly, they estimated how much funding that they needed to mobilise individually and agreed the specific timeframe within which such funds must be credited into an escrow account opened specifically for this purpose.

Afterwards, the Bank's recapitalisation funds, now in Disun's exclusive custody – and, up till that moment, at Doregos' disposal – would be transferred into an investment account in a third-party bank, where Doregos would be deprived of any opportunity of accessing the funds, should he, by some accident, get wind of Disun's activities, and, as would be expected, tried to act.

Once the Central Bank's re-capitalisation exercise kicked into full gear, Disun would pull these funds and systematically apply them towards mopping up the Bank's shares, using a legion of proxy companies and individuals. Doregos' funds would eventually be returned to his and the Bank's joint custody, or applied towards acquiring the Bank's shares according to a formula to be discussed and agreed with him in the future, sometime during the course of the recapitalization process. It was however important that Disun and Ige retained control until such a time when they became comfortable with their own positions, from which point they could gradually cede control of the "Doregos-funds" – or shares as they might be – back to the Bank. As Ige was quick to point out, the funds would be returned as and when they feel comfortable to do so. The bottom line according to Ige was the fact that they needed to hold on to the funds for as long as necessary as a bargaining chip and if need be, convert all or some of it, depending on how their scheme played out and how ugly the opponent – namely Jide Doregos – was willing to fight. This was the only aspect of the ensuing corporate manoeuvrings that Disun was not completely subscribed to, and whenever it came to that subject, he was always vehement in presenting his reservations.

"Well, Ige, you know that I wouldn't take what doesn't belong to me. I wouldn't convert somebody else's funds. These funds belong to Doregos or the Bank, depending on how you may want to look at it – in any case they aren't mine – I have no intention to convert these to my own use."

"You have to be realistic, Disun. At the end of the day, this is a takeover – a hostile takeover, if you may. If you understand it for what it really is, this, for all intents and purposes, is a war, and in a war situation, nothing is off limit. In the final analysis, our primary objective in this quest, is to win; and in realising this goal all tactics are permissible; all measures are worthy."

While they continued to seek consensus on the application of the "Doregos-funds" as they had now labelled it – each came up with his respective ideas on the likely sources of the initial leverage funding for the impending takeover.

Disun's strategy was to meet with Deroju Rogers and present her with a comprehensive proposal with respect to an investment plan in Quorum, facilitated by no one but himself, obviously, in which, for the benefit of a one-time investment of four-and-a-half billion naira into the Bank's recapitalisation effort, the Rogers would walk away with 25 percent of the Bank. Mr Dehinde Rogers would automatically assume the chairmanship of the Board, albeit as a figurehead, representing his as well as Disun's and Ige's interests. The real plan however was to utilise the Rogers' funds to acquire as many shares as would be necessary to ensure that Disun and Ige retained a clear majority – which remained a moving target, depending on how rigorously and aggressively the other players would be willing to fight to keep or enhance their respective positions. He would return the balance of the Rogers' funds at the end of the exercise, claiming limitations due to oversubscription and the Bank's resort to an inevitable share-allotment formula. The Rogers, of course, would feel initial resentment, but they would, at the end, find consolation in the Board Chairmanship, which would be reserved for their patriarch, come rain or shine.

Ige, for his part, decided that this would be a good time to transfer the bulk of his wealth in Chicago back to Lagos. What he did not reveal to his friend, however, was the fact that he was also the custodian of proceeds from an illicit trade involving some of his Columbian friends, which he had unilaterally decided to "invest" in Nigeria on their behalf. Warehousing millions of dollars for Columbian cartels was one thing; claiming to be investmenting this internationally on their behalf without their consent was another. Having lived and dealt with these men for so many years, Ige either knew he was doing, or was raving mad.

At the end of the evening, they had arrived at clear goals and timelines. The working mantra was "thirty million in three months" – thirty million American dollars, that is.

"It's that or nothing." Ige said, as he clouded the air with his cigar. "God is my witness."

Disun had never known Ige to be the religious type. His invocation of the Most High, for some reason, frightened the hell out of him.

CHAPTER 26

THE CHATTER FROM THE TV PRESENTERS on CNN sounded in his ears like the chirping of a few thousand birds; or the bickering of a hundred gibbons – anything but a healthy argument on the status of the United States economy, which indeed was what the commentators were having. He put the TV in mute, and as he rose from the sofa, his legs felt tired; heavy. He must have travelled a few kilometres on the soft Persian carpet of his Federal Palace Hotel suite, if the number of times he had paced up and down the entire length of the suite were anything to go by. He was at another of the Bank's Strategy Retreats for key executives, and, for various reasons, he simply just wasn't in the mood.

The monotony was gnawing at him like acid, seeping slowly, but devastatingly into every fibre of his psyche and crawling gradually into every crevice of his being. All attempts to improve his mood had fallen flat, and, as at that moment, he had lost all hope of being enlivened. Even then, it was an unusual kind of boredom, because, as he could tell from the throbbing of the taut, green vein, now sketched permanently on his temple like a little river, and the pool of moisture constantly gathering on his palms, he was, at the same time agitated. Rather uniquely, he was bored and restless at the same time.

Somehow, he recognised that this unusual tension was a symptom of something deeper – consequence of the internal turbulence that he was feeling. The pressure was pressing him down like the full weight of a mountain. But he was, at the same time, fearful. This confluence of feelings was unlike anything that he had previously experienced.

Perhaps, in a stranger aftermath, this tension was translating into an unusual desire, which, on the surface bore no correlation to its cause. The more he immersed himself in this coalescence of emotions, the more he longed for the company of a woman; indeed, if he were to be accurate in any way, the more he yearned for a feminine embrace. At first, this seemed a strange reaction to his disposition, since there was no obvious bearing between his circumstances and this nascent feeling. But then again, upon further consideration, he seemed able to find some rationale; or, at least, some plausible explanation. It was plausible that the anxiety-triggered violent pumping of his heart had inadvertently flushed blood to the peripherals – with the attendant, unplanned results; or it could be that the combination of so many conflicting emotions had resulted in a state of latent panic, triggering an infant-like instinct for maternal sheltering – perhaps the remnants of an evolutionary intuition fortuitously carried on into adulthood. Whatever the case was, the impulse was intense, and it seemed – rather decisively – that the pressures could only be suppressed by such comforts, as to which only a woman could provide. For several moments, Disun struggled to find a conclusive justification for his impulses. It was emotions such as these that had led great men to scandal. He was wise enough to realise that such feelings, if left untrained, could bring a man down. But then again – he rationed – these same impulses had brought some people up or down the social ladder, depending on where one had initially sat on the pyramid of life. For instance, what chance would a slave girl have had at the semblance of freedom, if not for the miracle of the mulato child that she had conceived within an instance of indiscretion at the peak of her masters lust. Or, how would the proletarian have had a fair chance at srengthening his generational blood with a bit of blue, had he not been caught off guard by the transgressing princess. Again, monumental follies such as these only occur when the normal functioning of the mind had been dampened by stress, distress or a coalescence of all of these; which then begs the question as to whether or not this is a deliberate scheme on Nature's part to foster a random chance at social mobility.

Disun quickly realised that he couldn't think himself out of his predicament. He knew that he had to address the prevailing tensions before they got the best of him. He might have to take up his pre-ordained role as an adjutant of Nature. In this reasoning, imperfect as it was, he must have finally found justification for his next act. This long-considered idea had finally found its time. He picked up the telephone and dialled the reception. Then he put the television in mute.

"Can you give me Ms Benny Asaju's room, please?"

There was a moment.

"Tell her it's Disun ..."

Another moment.

"Thank you."

Yet another moment, then the phone came alive on the other end and, upon hearing the expected voice, his face lightened up.

"Hi Benny. How are you?"

"So-so, Disun. I've been stuck in my room all day. Bored as hell."

"You must be reading my mind. That's exactly why I called you. I was wondering if you would like to have a drink. We can meet at the pool if it's okay by you."

"For sure. That would be nice."

"Ten minutes?"

"Come on now, a lady would need some time."

"Certainly. Pardon me. Half an hour then?"

"Half-an-hour should be fine."

"Okay, then. See you shortly."

Disun slipped into a pair of blue jeans, linen shirt and loafers, and stepped out of the room. Just as he was settling into a table-for-two, Abeni materialised at the huge ornate door that opened into the pool area. Disun could not take his eyes off her as she made her way towards the table, seeming to be floating across the marble floor as the gentle breeze of the evening licked her flowing silk gown, moving them around delicately around the contours of her body in an almost deliberate, dexterous manner. Abeni had a particular glow around her that moment that was intense, unfamiliar and mesmerizing at the same time.

"You look stunning," he said, as he rose and helped her into the empty seat opposite him.

"Thank you, Disun. You are very kind. You look quite well yourself."

"Well, I try. Thanks."

They ordered some drinks and after a few minutes of chitchat; their conversation acquired a serious edge.

"I'm sure you have been following the goings-on at the bank," Disun ventured.

"Who wouldn't," Abeni said. "Except one is not in the bank; or the industry for that matter. Even ordinary people are observing the events. Well, I would if I were they. People have got their life savings and retirement funds saved in these banks."

"It sure has been one tough couple of months."

"I'm sure it has. At your level, you have to be feeling the pressure directly."

"You can say that again…"

"And, not to mention the rumours that are currently making the rounds…"

"Well, tell me something new, Benny. You ladies have a way of staying ahead of the information pack."

"There is nothing I can tell you that you do not already know, Disun. Not at your level, and not with your industry connections."

"You may be surprised, darling. I could be as clueless as an ordinary office clerk, sometimes. One tend to get so engrossed in the daily grind, if one is not careful, one could easily lose touch of everything else."

"I see your point, Disun. But this time around, I'm sure you already know more than enough."

"Well, I suppose feigning oblivion would be futile, then."

"Trust me on that."

Their laughter was resounding.

"What might be news to you, however, is the fact that I may know a little more than I should."

"Well, Benny, very little would surprise me about you. You have your high-level associates and, if I we would be totally honest with each other, we must admit that you have your ways."

"Why do I have a sense that these statements are infused with hidden meaning?"

"Come on, Benny. You do have your ways. And I actually mean that as a compliment."

"Well, accepted, then. Thanks."

"Welcome. So, tell me what I don't know."

"You mean what we both know?" Abeni winked conspiratorially.

"Such as…"

"Such as the fact that you are poised to assume leadership of the Bank."

"What do you mean by 'you are poised to assume leadership of the Bank'? What in the world is such an incredible conjecture based on?"

"We know, Disun. At least those of us who need to know already know. We already know what is going on and it is a little late in the day to feign oblivion."

"Okay. Okay… I admit. There is actually no point feigning ignorance at this point. I am just so shocked that you know so much."

"We know what is going on. At least some of us do. And, guess what, we are all in your camp. We think you deserve this elevation. We would like to see you follow through."

Disun was silent for a while. He was dealing with several emotions at the same time: surprise and the need for honesty on the one hand; and, then, affection and, perhaps desire, on the other.

"Well, what can I say? I don't know if I deserve it or not, but I sure agree with you that I have a clear shot at this. What I don't know for sure is whether I want it or not."

"I think I can understand how you're feeling. At least, I can imagine that I do. With every life-changing opportunity comes an infusion of doubt. Doubt comes in small doses, then it grows. If you fail to nip it in bud, it becomes a monster. I could imagine that you suddenly feel empathy for the people on who's heads you might have to trample to get to your destination; you probably also worry about the prospects of resistance. The fear of the unknown brings unconscionable pain, understandably."

"Perhaps you really know more than you actually should, Benny, because you seem to be hitting the nail right on the head."

"But these are general facts. I just think that this is not the time for doubts, Disun. This is the time for resolve."

"I'm listening. "

"I'm glad you are, darling. This is your time. This is your appointment with destiny. Your concrete shot at greatness. This kind of opportunity comes once in a lifetime. If I were you, Disun, I will embrace it."

"I know you mean well, Benny. And I sincerely appreciate your inspiration. However, these things are easier said than done. It's a fierce, lonely battle to the summit, and, believe-you-me, once you're there, it even get's lonelier. Worse still, the only place to go is down."

"You shouldn't be entertaining such doubts at this particular point in time. Perhaps you haven't yet realised it, but this is your coronation…"

"Pardon me. "

"You are about to become the CEO of one of the top banks in the country, Disun. You are going to become one of the youngest CEOs in the industry. All things being equal, you have a fair chance at leadership. If you play your cards right, you could easily ascend to the throne."

"What throne, Benny. You are losing me now."

"The throne of the king, darling… King of Broad Street."

Disun felt a sudden rush of elation travel through his body like a buzz from a high-tension cable. He had no words in response. Only deep, silent contemplation.

"You have what it takes, and, at this very moment, you have a clear shot at ruling this industry. For someone coming from the gutters such as yourself – and please excuse my freedom in using such an expression, but I think I qualify to do so since I am from there myself – opportunities such as these come only once in a lifetime; once in several generations, perhaps. You need to think about all the young ghetto boys that would be inspired by you – by your success. All those young men and women who would wake up every morning and strive; just because they have heard your story; just because they have listened to your tale; read about you. All those thousands of kids who within your success would find a reason to fight. You cannot at this moment let them down."

"I know you are trying to inspire me, Benny, but would you be surprised if I slightly disagree with you? Being successful is one thing. Being an opportunistic wimp is another. To be sincere, I do not share your enthusiasm. Up till now, I believe I have earned every single *success* that I have."

"You could choose to accept what I am about to say or not, but at the least I know you would believe me when I say that I know a handful of so-called successful men intimately; I have been with some of these men at their most vulnerable. I have seen otherwise powerful men become what you call wimps. I have heard them confess to their fair share of "wimpiness", either at the depth of desire, or in a moment of drunken indiscretion. Beneath every successful man, Disun, is an opportunistic wimp. You may choose what it is that you want to believe but you know in the depths of your heart that I am saying the truth."

"For some reason, you're making me a little nervous, Abeni."

Abeni raised her glass-clutching hand, wagging her index finger with constrained anger. "You must be very nervous, indeed, since you just chose to call me by that reviled name. Never, ever again, under any circumstances should you call me that. That is a name stuck in my very distant past, and I have come a very long way since then. You are extremely privileged to have learnt of the name in the first place, and, especially, the place and time that it represents. I believe I can trust you not to repeat this error?"

Disun was shocked by Abeni's outburst and couldn't immediately find an appropriate response. What could have warranted such a vicious reaction? But, on a second thought, he reasoned that Abeni could still associate her village name with negativity: from her mother's long-term abuse, and from her experience with premature conception. Or, on the other hand, she could merely have been messing with his mind? Was she playing a mental game to disarm him and, then, slyly own him? He was completely at loss, but not sufficiently to be lost on the notion that he could never call her Abeni again. Not even in a moment of drunken indiscretion.

"You are making me even more nervous, Benny. Why flog a wounded horse."

"Nervous energy could be useful energy, darling, if only you know how to harness it."

"You seem to have all the right words tonight." Disun was mentally exhausted.

"Opportunism is part of living, in all sense; part of life; survival; victory! Would you ever win a game of chess by neglecting your opportunistic chances? In the jungle hierarchy, the Lion is King. I mean, would you call a lion that fed on a crippled zebra opportunistic? The Lion is King of the jungle for a reason."

"But, at the end, Benny, we are humans, not beasts."

"There is an animal in every one of us. At a time of disaster, in famine, at wartime, the animal in us all emerges. However, it is that small section of mankind who have learnt to channel this animalistic energy in peacetime that eventually wins. Have you ever tried to rationalise why the best of womanhood is often attracted to the worst of men? The answer is very simple: a ruthless man would do whatever is necessary to guaranty that he and his family do not only survive, but thrive. This is a pure evolutionary instinct. It may not be pleasant, but, darling, believe me, it is real."

"But then, what happens once you finally gain the world; rule the world as you have put it?"

Abeni leaned across the table, swiftly, jerkily and held Disun's hands in a tight grasp. "Then you will be king. You are destined to rule, Disun," she said in a quiet, raspy voice, staring him down with dark, crystal eyes. "You don't have to over-analysing it."

"Well, here you go again, Benny."

"You are the King of Broad Street, damn you! This is a coronation. Embrace it!"

Disun felt a sudden, violent jolt in his chest; then his heart picked up momentum. He felt warm blood rush into his temple. His eyes clouded with something that felt like tears; yet, he couln't ascertain the trigger for his emotions. His entire body began to tremble. His system seemed to be failing him.

"Are you going to objurgate, darling? Wake up and use your God-given brains. You only have one shot."

Disun struggled to pull himself together, fearing that he might lose whatever iota of his sovereignty that remained. For the first time that evening, he retuned her gaze with equal intensity, though he struggled to steady his hands. "I won't. I wont objurgate." The words came out instinctively: involuntarily. He could not determine how, or why.

"Do not shy away from your throne, Disun. Do not deny your destiny. If it helps, you can count on my support. I will be with you all the way. If it was so ordained, my intention is to be your queen."

Warm beads of perspiration broke out on Disun's forehead, even when the breeze drifting across from the swimming pool was freezer-cold. He was too flabbergasted to respond.

"You look tired," Abeni said, getting up, and pulling him up with her right hand, which, by the way, had been inter-twined in his all along. "You need to relax. Come with me. I know just how to make you comfortable."

As Disun rose from his seat, he tripped and nearly fell back into his chair. Then he grabbed the table and steadied himself. They walked away from the pool, side-by-side; in silence. For his part, Disun struggled to summon whatever remained of his senses. At the same time, he knew with certainty that he was heading into the deep, dark bowels of an uncharted territory. But, even then, he was far too exhausted to rationalise, nor resist the impulse. For the first time in a long time, he completely let go, and gradually eased himself into the dark welcoming depths of the great unknown.

CHAPTER 27

THE BUZZ CAME IN QUICK SUCCESSIONS – one after the other, seven times in a row. As he lay on the large leather sofa in one of the three living rooms of his Ikoyi mansion, Disun had been counting the calls as they came in. One every two or three minutes. Couldn't a man just catch a few moments of quiet sleep! As though the caller had heard his thought, there was a brief moment of reprieve. Then, as he drifted back into sleep, the phone begun to ring again, for the eighth time in a row.

At that juncture, he made a unilateral bet. If the phone rang for the eleventh time, he would have to answer the call. Five minutes later, the target had been met. Clearly, this caller was not about to let up. Disun rolled over, grumbled underneath his breath and just before it rang again, grabbed it.

It was an unknown number.

"Hello."

"Disun … " The voice on the other side said was familiar. "Disun … Disun … How many times have I called your name?"

It was Doregos. It was too late to hang up.

"Evening Sir," Disun said, flustered.

"You better say Good Evening to your head. Disun. Say good evening to your *Eleda*. And your Creator had better be on your side, because by the look of things, you may be saying Good Morning to Him soon."

"How are you, Sir?" Disun aimed to soften the tone of the conversation while buying precious, thinking time.

"Seriously? How am I? You really want to know how I am?"

Disun was petrified and relieved at the same time. At least, the expected reaction was coming through, only that he had no means of estimating what form it was going to take the next minute. "Just asking after your health, Sir."

"Really? You amuse me, Disun."

Disun knew better than to speak, at least, not for the moment.

"Even you, Disun. *Ti a ba ni omi lo maa se eja jina*…Who would have thought?"

Disun remained silent.

"*Asee kokoro ti o un j'efo, ara efo lo wa.*"

Disun remained silence, but with great effort.

"*Epa n pa ara e, o l'ohun n p'aja.*"

The silence continued, but barely.

"But really, what are you expecting to get out of this? What do you intend to gain?"

At that juncture, Disun knew that his scope for silence had lapsed. "I am indeed baffled by these proverbs, Sir. While I am an ardent student of the language, I struggle to find appropriate context for your proverbs … "

"May you be struck by thunder for the statement that you just made!"

"Excuse me, Sir?"

"You must be a bastard! Who do you think you are talking to?

"I am totally confused, Sir."

"You aren't confused yet. Indeed, you have only just begun."

Disun was too tense to speak.

"You have something of mine, Disun. You were entrusted with something of great value, and after confiding in you all these years… after raising you up from nothing, you choose to betray me like this? You choose to stab me in the back?"

"If only you would allow me to speak, Sir…"

"What do you have to say? What could come out of your mouth that would be of significance, you double-crossing piece of shit?"

"These are turbulent times, Mr Doregos," Disun didn't remember ever calling him that; perhaps he was compensating for something. "These are treacherous times. You are under great scrutiny from the Authorities. All eyes are on you and everybody wants your blood. All I have done is to anticipate the impending dangers and do what is right…what is prudent … proactively. Contrary to your insinuations, Mr Doregos, I have neither betrayed you; nor have I stabbed you in the back. All I have done is to stash things away in a safe place. Keep it safely until the tension subsides; till the pressure wears away. I would like to share all the information about the location of the funds with you, but that would be imprudent on my side. When the authorities clamp down, you may buckle. That way, we lose everything. But when the coast becomes clear, I will return to you what is rightly yours. I can understand that you are a bit apprehensive at the moment, but, Sir, on that fateful day, you will thank me."

"You better pray to your God that you are around to see that day!"

"Pardon me, Mr Doregos, but I missed your last comment."

"You're damned right you did, you back-stabbing bastard. You think you know all about me, don't you? You think you have me all figured out? You don't even know the half of it, you insolent son-of-a-gun. If you have any real intelligence, you would have realised that there has to be more to this guy than meets the eye, given all his accomplishments – against all the odds. I think you are about to come into cognisance with the facts – first hand. I think you are about to be introduced to the real Doregos."

"I'm going to pretend I didn't hear that, Sir, but by all indications, you appear to be threatening me. Those could be legitimate grounds to press charges – "

"With what you just got yourself into, you bastard, even the law would not be able to save you … even the law will keep their distance from you. This is war. With the war that I am fighting with my persecutors, there are rules … there are ground rules. There are lines that could not be crossed. But with little backstabbing filths such as yourself, anything, and, indeed, everything goes. If you knew anything about history, you would realise how filthy scums like yourself have fared. I need not say more."

The phone went dead with a click.

"Haba, Disun. Come on now. I can't believe you're panicking like this."

"Please quit the drama, Ige. There's no panicking anywhere. Nonetheless, I wouldn't sit down here and pretend that everything is fine. Doregos is a dangerous man."

They were seated in one of the ground floor living rooms at Disun's house – the one overlooking the expansive garden and swimming pool at the back of the house. Disun's resident chef had prepared a banquet of assorted meats: chicken; goat; beef – grilled, fried, stir-fried – and he had supplied an equally diverse collection of drinks for them to enjoy and critique. Ige was digging deep into the banquette, but Disun seemed uninterested.

"Well, for your information Mr Disun, so am I. I can excuse your innocence. Naturally, you're inclined to forever see me as the Ige with whom you roamed the streets of Makoko many years ago. I can understand that, and I would rather not distort that blissful memory that we share. But, that was a long time ago. The Ige that is now sitting before you is a changed man. Believe it or not, if this were Chicago, I guarantee you that you will receive a phone call from Doregos first thing tomorrow morning recanting every vile word that he had spoken to you and apologising profusely."

"Incidentally, Ige, we are in Lagos. You are in the wrong territory. People like Doregos have an army of suicide men on contract. They have key law-enforcement people on their payroll. They have a section of the judiciary in their pocket. They would go to any length…"

"Let them bring the worst of their anger to bear, Disun. Let them summon the vilest of their demons. We aren't sleeping. And keep in mind Doregos is a sinking man. This is common knowledge. All his boneheaded goons far and wide are aware of this fact. They aren't stupid. Doregos' powers are diminishing by the day."

"But we also know that a sinking man is a dangerous man; he has nothing to lose."

"We won't be caught napping, Disun. I am not sleeping. I have been hard at work since this whole thing begun. I am already making provisions. I am covering all grounds."

"Tell me what you're doing."

"Well, if you would step outside with me for a moment … "

They made their way through the myriad of living rooms and foyers and once they were on the front porch, Ige ushered his friend to the side of the building were a parade of vehicles were lined up underneath the pavilion that was made to shield Disun's cars from the elements.

"I didn't realise that you came in a convoy." Disun said, not knowing what to make of the spectacle before him.

"Well, my intention was to save this till I was on my way out, but since you brought up the topic—"

Disun could not hide his astonishment as he gaped at the parade of vehicles before him. There were three vehicles line up side-by-side. The first was a brand-new, police-standard Toyota Hilux pick-up truck, painted a dull military-black and with its windows tinted all through. All four doors were open, flaunting the armed policemen seated inside. The policemen stepped out once Ige and Disun approached them and stood at attention. The second car was a Mercedes Benz G550 SUV, also black and tinted. This had a uniform driver standing by the passenger side, using a piece of soft leather to wipe off fingerprinted blemishes from the gleaming paintwork every once in a while. The third was another Hilux pick-up truck, same colour and details as the first, only that this was manned by two men, who, in their dark, navy-blue uniform resembled policemen, but whom were, by all indications, operatives of a private security outfit.

"This is your new entourage," Ige said. "All handpicked. The officers are among the best that the Force could offer and the privates are from the number-one firm. Your driver is also from the same outfit. Do not be deceived by their calm demeanour. These are top-notch bodyguards with many years of experience protecting important politicians, government officials, top celebrities and billionaires. These are men steeped in Marshall Arts and in the use of a broad range of standard and improvised weapons. Not only that, they have all been tested in the most dire of situations and they all came out tops; therefore we can comfortably say that they are all tried, tested and trusted. You have to be extremely influential and well connected to pull together an elite team such as the one that we have assembled, and not to mention extremely liquid. Luckily, we aren't deficient in either jurisdiction. And, we have enough justification to go all out. The VIP in question is not only extremely valued, but also extremely loved."

"You never cease to amaze me, Ige."

"Well, of what use would this maestro be?

"But then, do we really have to go this far?"

"It all depends on your perspectives. But, then again, let's go back into the house; we can continue this discussion once inside," they begun to make their way back. "Are you really ready to play this game? If the answer to that question is 'yes', then there are no two ways to go about it. The truth is that whether you like it or not, you are already playing the game. Except you are decisive, the game would play you. You see, people like Doregos are bullies – mere opportunistic sharks that thrive on the weakness of their victims. They seek you out, test your mettle and once they sense weakness, tread on you. Piss on you, if you let them – you may want to pardon my French – but the minute they come into contact with real steel – real resolve; the minute they are met with tangible resistance, they capitulate, retreat and flee. How many like Doregos have we met on the Streets of Chicago? How many like Doregos have we vanquished?"

"Hmnnnnnn…" Disun could only sigh.

"Granted, Doregos is a devil. But, guess what, he is a devil that we know."

Debo remained mute.

"I guess the all-important point is that you cannot be held back by someone like Doregos. Granted the devil that he is, it is on record that the devil flees in the face of defiance. We need to show strength, not weakness."

"And if Doregos were the devil, what does that make us?"

"It appears that there is still a part of you that remains wedded to this fictitious notion that you have a fair shot at greatness, eh? That you have a fair chance? Indeed, there is nothing like a truly fair chance, only that the odds are better in some societies than others, and, perhaps, in every society, within certain classes. The reality – as we both know it – is that you and I, unfortunate as it may sound, neither belong to the right society nor to the right class. So, the question, therefore, is, what are you arrested by? Your perceived sense of morality; your need for rationalisation or the prospect of great achievement – pure and simple?"

"I am driven by the realisation of the common good? And, in the process, my retention of some of spiritual congruency."

"You worry too much, Disun. You're a very sensitive guy. You agonise on things over which you have very little control. Little things, I call them. The only way to succeed in this life, is to focus the bulk of one's energy on the here and now. If I were you, I will concentrate on the tangible. I will focus on what I can control."

"Your world-view is getting stranger by the day, Ige. I say this without prejudice, and I believe you have enough reason to trust my intentions; but, honestly, I think you may be losing your mind."

"You're damned right I may be, Disun. Guess what, you're damned right I am! You think this is only about you? You think this struggle is only about you? Just in case you do not realise it, this battle is greater than you, Disun. This struggle is about the destiny of a generation. Whether you admit it or not, you have been entrusted with the opportunity of a million men. Whether you like it or not, you are the custodian of a million hopes. Right or wrong, this is the vantage card that providence had dealt you. What do you want to do: squander it?"

"That's beside the point, Ige. The key issue for me concerns the morality of this plan."

"Well, that indeed, is the point? What is the morality in giving banking licenses to a select few to milk everyone else dry and feed fat on statutory "manna"? Where is the morality in poverty, helplessness; hopelessness for all the other scroungers? What is the morality in the fact that many children go to bed daily, hungry, while their fathers are tending to the lives and properties of people who constantly throw surplus food in the bin? What is the morality in watching a grown man cry out or desperation and despair?"

"Here we go again, Disun. I can see that you have found yourself another odd tangent to go off on."

"Okay. Tell me: Have you ever witnessed a man cry?"

"Well, of course I have. Haven't we all? For instance, I remember once finding my father sobbing quietly in the outhouse; two in the morning, several hours after he and my mother had summoned me into their bedroom and informed me that they could not afford to finance my university education. It was a terrible thing to behold. I still get goose pimples till today, just thinking about it."

"I have witnessed this more than once; and I have seen men cry, not out of grief or bereavement, but out of despair. I have seen grown men weep out of sheer hopelessness and defeat. Tell me, what is the morality in that? On every occasion, it had been one of the most harrowing experiences I have ever had. It isn't something that you could ever get used to. It affects you from the core; and it affects you for life. But then, there is even something worse than watching a man cry…"

"Hmnnnn. Tell me."

"Watching a soul cry."

For a moment, Disun merely gawked in quiet contemplation. Then he nodded in affirmation. "I think I understand what you are referring to here."

"I'm sure that you do, Disun. I'm sure that you have witnessed the crying of a soul. I'm sure you would recognise the weeping of a distraught, vibrant soul, looking for an anchor of any kind; something to hold on to and leverage off out of the doldrums; out of downright dejection. It's a delicate find. You have to pay close attention, otherwise, you may not recognise it for what it truly is. I have witnessed my fair share of weeping souls, Disun. I see them all the time. I see them in the youth. In Makoko. Everywhere. A weeping soul makes no sound? The weeping is in deep silence. You could only observe it; perhaps, only perceive it. You see it in the furrows on the brows; the constant edge in the voice; the studious swagger of seeming insolence; the vanquish-defying-strut. Every once in a while – within that rare, spontaneous moment of attentiveness – you capture the silent sobbing in your mind's eye; you hear it in your sub-consciousness. And, sometimes it presents itself as a desperate bellowing wail.

"A yelling, often in panic, which – in the same vein – you could only hear with your mind's ear. You must have witnessed the stern, resolute countenance of the hapless, as he stands at the bus stop – bogus briefcase in hand, phantom mission on mind; or the studied swagger of a man going nowhere; just an important mirage that he had created in his now-troubled psyche, to engage mind and muscles just for that one moment; something to distract from an imminent meltdown. Perhaps you have witnessed the defiant plastic smile on a hopeless face, a tiny streak of sunshine at the tip of an iceberg of despair. You may have witnessed the wide, deathlike grin of a sinking man, achieving nothing but a grimace as he makes a half-hearted bid at hiding a pointless existence behind the façade of dry, self-degrading humour. I don't know about you, but I see these faces all the time; people – men, women, children – who have lost all hope, yet struggling to hang on to the final remnants of their pride.

"It is even worse with the elders. With them, it is a much-deeper crying. It is the quiet sob of a dying soul. For then, the battle is already lost. In them, you see an empty, hollowed-out soul confronted by an imminent demise. I see them all the time – even in the forgotten alleys of Chicago. Homeless folks pushing along their battered carts, lost, forlorn faces; wandering around for hours at a time. The main difference is that, these folks stand a chance. We have heard stories of those mongst them who had turned around to become millionaires, just as many had become maestros. The same cannot be said of our folks over here. Our society provides no such leverage. Except, however they choose to trade whatever remained of their battered soul for a slice of the good life. These are those who, in their desperation, choose to cross to the other side; the darker side. Without the courting of evil, they stand no chance. These are men who have been brought to their mental knees. I call them the walking dead. For these, there are no new beginnings. Just, simply, the end."

"But who says there is only evil to be courted as a legitimate exit from despair? What happened to the courting of Grace?"

"Tell you what, Grace envelops the world. Grace is the ultimate blanket. But how many of our people truly have the confidence to submit themselves to its workings? How many are willing to surrender to the discipline that elevates faith; how many could lead the lifestyle that pays credence? Even these people in their perceived ignorance understand the workings of supernatural things. Having led a lifetime devoid of the tenets, they are, as you would expect, reluctant to submit. But then again, there are a few that truly and genuinely flourish. Some, who in spite of monumental adversity insulate themselves with faith. In their souls, you would never see a weeping. But these are few and far between."

"Well, even when I don't always agree with you, I could appreciate your logic. You have always tended to have a more pessimistic view than I; and I am not surprised that you have carried on with that perspective even up till today."

"Well, I have a fundamental belief that every law-abiding citizen – man, woman and child – is entitled to a minimum level of dignity which the State ordinarily has the moral and statutory obligation to provide. However, where society has made nonsense of this duty, many have lost hope. Yet, many more have made it their prerogative to device an alternative means. We have a responsibility, Disun. You, especially, carry a unique burden considering what you represent to these people. A million youths are looking up to you. Perhaps tens of million of them. Even if, at the end, your perceived success is a fallacy, it is worth attaining if only for the sake of these kids. In your success, they might develop a perception of a fairer chance. In this perception, they might find inspiration towards the straight path."

"But then we would have lived a lie; and these kids would even be devastated if they ever found out the truth."

"The salient word is 'if', which you can be rest assured that they never would. There is no pure, crystal clean success story out there. What is presented is the cleaned-out version. If you ever get the chance to peal the layers, you would be amazed. My brother, *Isale oro, o l'egbin.*"

"You never change, Ige. But, then again, I hear you."

"I never will. You can literally take that to the bank."

Mama Disun surfaced in the dinning room with the last tray of her breakfast banquet in her hands. Even in her old age, no one made boiled yam, omelette and tea as well as she did. At least so her family thought, even when the era of the *carnation* brand was long gone and now replaced by a multitude of brands from all across the world. As she set the last tray on the table, she begun to arrange the tea condiments – milk, sugar, lime – and once her husband had started to help himself, she settled down beside him and joined in.

Also at the table were Olumide, his wife and his two daughters. Even with their demanding routines, family breakfast every Saturday morning was something that was constant and despite her retinue of domestic staff, Mama Disun chose to do most of the cooking and, indeed, the heavy lifting herself. This must have been her way of staying active and alert. The family adored her for this.

Breakfast went on quietly, with the exception of the morning news that was broadcasting from the living room TV, and Baba Disun's intermittent paraphrasing, since only he had a direct line of sight to the TV by virtue of his vantage positioning on the dining table. There was also the quiet chattering of the domestic maids living with the family who sat at the kitchen table, also having their breakfast. As unusual, Baba Disun's commentary, following the sequence of TV programming, would shift from politics, to the economy and then sports – and his perspectives would remain stern and serious, but only until Olumide would interject with a comical remark and the table would erupt in thunderous laughter. Even the maids joined in, often failing in their attempt to cover up their eavesdropping. For the most part, everything was normal, but only until heavy knocking at the door startled them.

"Who's that?" Baba Disun ventured. "Are we expecting anyone?"

"Not necessarily," Olumide said, voicing the blank looks on everyone's faces. "I'll see who's there."

Olumide approached the door and just as he turned the handle, the door flung open and three men rushed into the living room, all masked, and all bearing weapons.

"Baba! Where's Baba?" one of them yelled. "Where's Baba?"

"Who are you?" Olumide rebuffed, standing his ground and making to obstruct the men's progress into the house. He switched to a more aggressive, pidgin tone. "*Wetin you want? You no go fit come here dey harass* ..."

The lead marauder's fist connected with the centre of Olumide's jaw and, that instance, he was knocked out cold. One of the men stood over him with the muzzle of his AK-47 rifle pointing down at his face. The other two made their way towards the dinning area.

They arrived at the dinning room to meet Baba Disun alone at the table. The rest of the family had scamperred into the house, leaving him at the head of the table where he had been having his meal. Indeed, had it not been for the preceding commotion, everything would have seemed normal. Baba Disun had seen the men as they came in, and he had seen the violence that they had unleashed on his son. As the men approached his table, he stood up and as he begun to speak the leader of the gang motioned to him to sit down and keep quiet.

"Gentlemen " Baba Disun attempted to speak once again.

"I said keep quiet!" The man placed a silencing finger across his lips. "Silence. I do all the talking from now on. You only speak when I ask you to speak. You only answer my questions."

"Well noted, my son," Baba Disun said, "May God bless ..."

"Shut your mouth," without warning, the gang leader dug the butt of his gun into the older man's chest. "Let that be the last time that anything will come out of your mouth until I ask you to speak. By the way, I am not your son. You know who your sons are, and, to be honest, one of them is the very reason that we are here today. Your other son is lying face down on the floor over there. Those are your sons. *We* are your masters. If I were you, I will show some respect."

"What do you want, gentlemen? "

The rifle butt came down hard on the old man's ribcage once again. "I said shut up! You only speak when I ask you to. You only answer my questions!"

"I am Sorry..." Baba Disun said, doubling over and coughing violently.

"That's better. Just so you know, you are coming with us."

"I do not understand, gentlemen..."

"You will in a moment. Bundle him!"

The third thug approached Baba Disun and begun to rough-handle him.

"Take it easy, young man. You can take anything you want from the house. There are valuables, jewellery, cash. Anything that you may want. But asking me to come with you is completely unnecessary. Whatever the issue is, we could resolve it amicable…we could resolve it here…"

The gang leader let out an unruly laugh. "Imagine! The old man is negotiating with us?" He laughed again. "You had better behave yourself, Baba. Otherwise, we shoot you in both ankles and carry you like a Christmas goat. I believe I have given you sufficient introduction to our goal. If you continue to resist, we may not be able to control ourselves. *Oya!* You bundle the man out!"

Gangster number three begun to shove Baba Disun towards the door, just as Olumide came round and struggled to make out what was going on around him. The clubbing of his minder's gun jolted him back into oblivion. Once Baba Disun had been pushed out of the house, Mama Disun and the rest of the family rushed into the living area and begun to yell out for help. As Mama Disun made her way towards the exit, she stumbled on her son and fell flat on the floor. Olumide's wife fell over her and so did the maids. Then Mama Disun managed to get on her feet again, dashing towards the door and yelling at the top of her voice.

The rattle of sub-machine guns rends the air as Mama Disun broke through the door into the open. She ducked back into the house in one quick swooping movement. Then she lay crouched on the floor, as did everyone else. Olumide was regaining consciousness at the moment, but his wife laid on him, pinning him down with her body. She had a mobile phone pressed against her face and she was talking to someone whom she was referring to as "Commodore". Mama Disun was praying beneath her breath. The maids sobbed quietly.

Ige's mobile phone ran frantically.

"Hello…"

"Ige! The worst has happened! Ige… Ige."

"What happened, Disun? Calm down."

"They have taken Daddy … They have my dad!"

"What do you mean they have your dad? Who? How?"

"I don't know Disun. It just happened. Not quite half-an-hour ago. I understand that some thugs just showed up at the house. They overpowered the guards, beat Olumide up and grabbed the old man. Nobody knows who they are, but then, who else could they be? We already know who could be responsible for this."

"Well, let's settle down, Disun. Let's try to understand what is going on. Where are you now?"

"I am heading to Makoko as we speak. I am on the way to the house."

"Any word from the people? Any requests. Any claims?"

"Nothing. I said it has only been thirty-minutes; an hour at most. I learnt that the kidnappers made their escape by the lagoon. They had speedboats. However, I was also told that the neighbourhood youths gave them a chase. Risked their lives. That's the part that touched me the most. But Olumide's wife also called her uncle – the Commodore – who called up someone senior in the Navy. There is a lot of information coming through; and it's all coming through at the same time, so I am doing my best to make sense out of it all. In any case, what remains clear is that my father is at the mercy of some thugs somewhere…all because of me."

"Well, again Disun, we cannot jump to any conclusions yet. There is wholesale kidnapping all across the country as we all know. These could just be a bunch of opportunistic goons looking for an easy buck. Son's a top-notch banker; dad lives in relative freedom in Makoko: It's a no-brainer."

"I sure appreciate your effort at calming me down, Ige. Thanks; but, indeed, no thanks. In spite of your best effort – and I know you mean well – it sure is a no-brainer. This has Doregos' signature written all over it."

"Well, I hear you, Disun…I hear you. Let's observe and act. I have a few phone calls of my own to make. Do let me know when you get to Makoko and keep me posted as things unfold. If you would still be there within the hour, I will join you. If you have to leave, let me know where you'll be. Whatever the case, I will be with you within an hour."

"For sure."

"Don't worry, Disun. We'll get to the bottom of this... And Dad will just be fine. You can trust me when I say that."

"Well, I guess I'll talk to you in a bit."

"OK then."

"OK."

As Disun hung up his phone, he heard the phone beep as a text message came in. The sender was unregistered on his phone and the number was unrecognisable. He taped on the green button to retract the text.

"A ta koro wo'nu ado, ko le mu omo inu e woo... He who magigally spins into a gourd...cannot take his son along – nor his father, for that matter."

His heart seized in an instance; and then, the very next instance, it felt as though a thousand elephants were standing on it.

CHAPTER 28

THE SIX-CAR CONVOY CRUISED GENTLY through the back roads of Ikoyi, keen to avoid the bustling Lagos traffic, which could be unrelenting, even on an otherwise tranquil Sunday afternoon. While the police truck at the head of the convoy was equipped with sirens and flashlights, the occupant officers knew not to deploy these without clear approval from their boss. The reality as it turned out was that this approval had only been given twice, the first instance being on an urgent trip to pick up the boss and ferry him to the airport on time to catch an international flight – on which occasion the boss was not in convoy as the cars blared their sirens and sped through the traffic. The other was only six months ago, as they meandered through the irate Friday traffic, leading a much longer convoy of mourners to the Ikoyi cemetery. The boss was in the convoy on that occasion, sitting in the passenger seat by the uniformed driver of the hearse, glancing occasionally at the iron casket behind them.

Even as they travelled on the same route this Sunday afternoon, the siren-baring vehicles knew not to deploy the emblems of their authority on this occasion. Everyone knew that the boss was still at odds with the trappings of office. The boss was a reluctant initiate into the lifestyle of the Nigerian economic elite. The convoy drove into the open gates of the cemetery and pulled up, one after the other, by the main channel. Disun stepped out of the Mercedes Benz G550 and Ige appeared right beside him. Two of the cemetery attendants materialised from thin air, and after a minute of pleasantries, Disun and his friend begun to make their way through the main channel to the narrower pathways that would lead them to the grave. The attendants were one step ahead, directing and clearing small obstacle of fallen branches out of the way. The rest of the entourage maintained a respectful distance behind them.

It was a bright, sunny morning, which was helpful, given the sheer melancholy in the air. It also helped that the breeze was cool, fresh and gentle and also that an orchestra of birds where churning out their songs. At the end, cemeteries where enhanced with natural beauty for a reason. While he would rather not be there in the first place, on this occasion, Disun gave his thanks. They trekked quietly for a few minutes through a parade of ornate marble and granite tombstones – marking the final resting places of heroes, villains and bystanders long passed – and after sojourning well into the depths of the cemetery, they arrived at their destination, in a secluded, reserved section of the grounds. Though the adjourning flowers had grown and flourished, and though the grave's bed had been receptive to a sprinkle of fallen leaves, the black granite stones and the golden prints that eulogised the occupant was familiar.

Mr. Adeduntan Alade Falodun

12th January 1940 – 6th of March 2004?

May His Soul Rest In Peace

If Disun's long gaze at the prints was anything to go by, he could have been seeing them for the first time. Then, gazing at the golden cursive prints as they were carefully etched on the glazed surface of the granite, his vision suddenly blurred. Then the lettering disappeared, and, eventually, the entire grave went with it. He reached in his jacket and retrieved a crisp white handkerchief with which he wiped his eyes. The lettering came to light only for another moment, before his eyes welled up, and his vision was once again blurred. It had been six months since the old man died, and it had taken him that long to finally bring himself back to the grave. It had been six agonizing months.

As he stood there, gazing at his father's grave and muttering intermittent prayers, he couldn't stop hearing the doctor's voice playing back in his mind as the latter broke the devastating news to him:

I am really sorry, Mr Falodun. We did absolutely everything that we could.

As he was to learn afterwards, the neighbourhood boys had given the kidnappers a chase, cornering them at a jetty and engaged them in a gun duel. During the commotion, Baba Disun had escaped into the lagoon and swam for half an hour before he was recued. The old man was however already in great danger by the time he was rescued. He had suffered a heart attack, which his rescuers could neither recognise nor address. By the time Baba Disun was brought to the hospital, it was too late.

When they finally turned away from the graveside and started making their way through the gardens and tombstones to the cars, the sun had descended, the weather was cold and the earlier singing of the birds had given way to the chirping of a few, early-bird bats. The bright and sunny atmosphere that greeted them upon their arrival had now yeilded to a gray, downcast gloom, and so was the mood of the departing men.

Disun shook his head as they progressed, and then, suddenly, dropped his head. Ige patted him on the back, keeping uncharacteristically silent.

"A son never ceases to mourn his dad," Disun murmured, still shaking his head.

"I understand."

The drive back to Disun's house was short, since their back-road track had been left unclogged, thankfully, and once they had settled into the comforts of his living room and was awaiting dinner, Ige poured himself a drink.

" I truly understand where you are, Ige. If anyone does, then that person, certainly, *is* me. I however also understand a fundamental fact of life, which I believe, essentially, that we both agree on. And that is the fact that real vision never sleeps; real vision never grieves."

"True. I mean, some of the greatest men in history have met with great calamity... sometimes at the peak of their calling; sometimes at the most vital moments of their quest... the onus had always been on them to summon their innermost strengths and, with a bit of fortitude, pull through."

"That's the thing about you; you have been endowed with wisdom like a sprouting spring. You could already anticipate where I am going with this. Perhaps this is why we are friends in the first place. Perhaps this is why we have remained friends for so long "

"I hear you… Ige. What more can I say? But, on the other hand, truth-be-told, this so-called-vision is wearing me out. Honestly, Ige, I am tired."

"Well, I really appreciate how you feel; particularly, how you're feeling this very moment, Disun. I mean, who wouldn't? But what is the responsible thing to do? That is the big question. What is the proper thing to do? Whether I like it or not, you would be well within your rights and you would be acting within a fair measure of reason if you said that you were ready to quit right now. But, then, looking at it from another perspective, would I be acting responsibly if I let you. Would I be living up to the man that I have always claimed I am if I let you back down at this crucial moment? Would you be the man that we both know that you are, if you did? You've already sacrificed a lot, Disun. You've already given so much. It's too late to turn your back now. This is not the time to waiver. This is the time to follow-through. I however need to know where you stand. At the end, this is entirely going to be your call?"

"What is the implication of this 'call', Ige. What more is this game going to require from me? What more is this game going to *take* from me?"

"I'm not entirely clear, Disun. I guess I am a bit fuzzy from this drink; but what exactly are you thinking. There is something that is playing at the back of your mind that you haven't said."

"I need to know what I am getting myself into this time, if I commit to going forward. What more do I have to lose? What more do I have to give?"

"But we already have everything laid out. We have it all together. There is nothing left for us to do but to execute. All we need now is the courage to stand firm and follow through. Except I am mistaken, there is all that there is to it… there is nothing more to give."

"You lie, Ige. For the first time in our friendship, you are looking me in the eyes and lying to me. You have lied to me a thousand times before; perhaps I have lied to you a few hundred. We have both lied to each other on the most trivial of things; things that are of little or no consequence. The grave issue is really not that you are lying to me at this particular point in time or not; it is that you are lying on something so monumental … and, the most scary part of it is that you are looking me straight in the eyes. This is something that you have never done. This is what baffles me."

"Okay, what do you want from me, Disun. What do you want me to say? I am doing this for both of us. I'm trying to be strong."

"I do not dispute that, Ige. But you still haven't answered my question. My question remains: What more do I have to lose? What more do I have to give?"

"Okay, since you want us to go that route, then being evasive would be futile. So, how do you want this? The good news first or the bad news?"

"Pick your choice."

"Okay, so I'll take the bad news first; then, the good."

Disun shrugged. Ige re-filled his glass and downed it.

"There is no need to sugar-coat this, is there?" Ige paused for a long moment, holding his friend in an icy gaze. "The bad news is that you've got nothing left to give but your soul." He paused meaningfully. "The good news, however, is that this doesn't cost a dime; and better still, it is a one-time trade; a once-and-for-all stance. All you have to do is to make up your mind."

"Is this a proposition?"

"Disun, I know that your dad just passed, and I recognise the pain that comes with that experience, especially, given the bond that you guys shared. I also have to congratulate you, because, in the end, you had a father who was present, and you shared a pretty decent relationship with him, and, therefore, lots of cherished memories. Mine was a fairly different experience. While my father is still alive to the rest of the world, to me, he had never been. He had always been someone that existed in the peripherals of my mind and he had always been in the fringes of my life. I had learnt to live as though he weren't there and as I grew up, I did something resourceful. I found new fathers for myself. I have them in every town, every city, every country that I have been; precisely, every country that I have lived in. Call then mentors; call them godfathers – if you like – call them my spiritual leaders. Call them what you want. The bottom line is that I have these people on my side … and they all bring something to the table. Some bring connections; some bring powers –

social… political… spititual. Thankfully, I have some of them in Lagos, and, one particularly comes to mind as we speak. If you have an hour, we can take the short drive outside the City. The elders say that it is he who hadn't been confronted by war that fashions himself as a man. I can understand your fears, your apprehension. You are very weak at the moment; very feeble. I can understand that that is where all this anxiety is coming from. But I also recognise what we need to do. What we need to do is to strengthen you. Strenghten your spirit. Fortify you. I think we should visit this Baba as soon as possible.

"So, I presume then, hopefully without sounding cheeky, that this is the first step in the preternatural "selling-of-my-soul", then?"

Ige made a silent, noncommittal motion, which was followed by a long pause, punctuated only by the muffled bickering of the political analysts on CNN, filtering in from the TV in one of the adjacent living rooms.

After a few minutes, Disun sighed heavily. When he spoke, his tone was quiet, reflective. "I can infer that your key point – judging by all this – is that having come this far, it has to be sink-or-swim from now on, then?"

Ige made another evasive gesture, but he spoke this time. "Well, if you want to look at it that way."

An eternity of silence followed. Finally, Disun broke the silence.

"Really, what is there to lose, other than that which you have just defined?"

Ige rose from his chair, leaned on the head of the chair and smiled a little. "I think you now see the point."

But his celebration was prematurely cut short once Disun spoke again.

"Do you ever contemplate the Aftermath of all this though?"

"You mean, after we have pulled through with the plan and you have assumed your the leadership of Quorum Bank? What else could happen? We would have the whole world beneath our feet. Broad Street would be ours for the taking!"

"You just said it's sink-or-swim; do-or-die, didn't you?"

"Yes."

"So, what I mean is: what happens, if or, perhaps, more accurately, *when* we – well, for want of a better expression – eventually die?"

Disun was deeply astonished by Ige's lack of spontaneity. Perhaps for the first time in their friendship, Ige did not have a clever, eloquent response.

"Well, I guess death would take care of itself," He said, finally. "We can only worry about what we can control. All we can reasonably care about is the here and now."

"Okay then, I suppose I will reflect deeply on this over the next couple of days. We may have a trip to make together this weekend."

"That's it! Now you're on the right track, Disun. We're almost there..." Ige's statement was covertly vague, encouraging split interpretation of his insinuation on progress as referring to the clandestine taking over of Quorum Bank, or, serendipitously, the imminent scarification of a soul.

The conversation steadily diminished through the remaining hours of the night, until Disun begun to doze off, and Ige, with his friend's permission, took his leave.

The vision came with a torrent of lights, filtering through in shimmering streaks of red, orange, yellow and white. It resembled a fiery soup of molten heat, bubbling in the crater of a volcano, or, on the fiery surface of Mars. It was a familiar scene and his typical response, from experience, was, simply, to open his eyes, and brace up for the impact. When he did, the sudden surge of brightness was blinding. The few errant rays that were slicing through the partitions in the damask blinds shone directly on his face. He sat up jerkily, and doubled over on his haunch. Then he wiped his hand over his face. He had been passed out on the couch, all through the night.

This was nothing unusual, since, there had been many nights before then when, having stretched every single fibre in his muscles, twined a few of his nerves and killed some of his brain cells in his quest to prepare for the future – while barely surviving the day – he had arrived at his mansion, deep into the night, shattered. Recognising, on such nights, the futility of his proper bedtime routine, the generous sofa in his most private living room had always been his refuge. And, as his domestic staff had come to understand whenever this transpires, he was never to be disturbed. They also knew to always leave the television in the adjacent room on, as the boss detests a silent house. This was, perhaps, a trait carried on from his Makoko days, where there was never a dull moment, not even in the wee hours of the morning. Coming from that background, living in a five-bedroom mansion with a half-dozen speechless staff, could be daunting. The staffers, however, were oblivious to the intuition for their boss's seemingly unusual behaviour; but consistent with their own custom, they never asked.

Disun got off the sofa and made his way past the adjacent living room – where the same set of political commentators were still yakking away on CNN, in an apparent repeat broadcast of the previous night's show – then past the dinning area where his chef had arranged what seemed like a sumptuous meal. He smiled a faint contented smile. What would a poor bachelor like him have done without the services of his reliable staff! With the fear and tension all around him, it was satisfactory to know that his home, at least, remained a sanctuary.

A quick dash up the stairs to his bedroom and he was soon back at the breakfast table, tidy, clean and wide awake. Not feeling particularly hungry, he grabbed a platefull of snacks and made his way to the adjourning living room were the television had been on all night. At the moment, CNN was broadcasting a documentary on Conspiracy Theories, which was a topic that Disun had always been interested in. This was a welcome distraction, and he settled deep into the couch as he dug into the snacks beside him. The day was building up to a good start.

Then, suddenly, one of his mobile phones came alive.

Disun ignored it. This was uncharacteristic behaviour on his part, but he was too immersed in the tranquillity of that morning to be bothered by any distractions. Whoever didn't respect his Saturday mornings deserved no such respect from him, he thought. All calls could wait for now. At his convenience, he would return the calls as necessary.

Then the phone rang again. Then, again.

He stretched over and picked it up. It was Abeni.

He smiled. And to think that he hadn't been interested in picking up the phone!

"Benny," he rearranged himself mentally. "Benny, how are you?"

"Disun! Disun! Is your TV on?"

"Yes it is, Benny. What's going on?"

"Put on your TV, Disun. Put your TV on!"

"My TV is on, Benny. I thought I just said that. What's going on? Calm down."

"What channel is it one?"

"CNN."

"Tune to a local channel, Disun. Tune to Lagos TV."

"Okay, I am doing so as we speak, but what's the matter, Benny. You don't sound right."

"It is unbelievable, Disun. I am in shock. I am completely at loss. I really can't talk where I am. I've got to go now. I will call you back shortly. Or, I will just come over to the house. This really cannot be happening."

"Benny; Benny, hold on…"

Abeni was gone.

Disun grabbed the TV remote control and flipped rapidly through the channels until he found Channel seven. The seven o clock news was on, but nothing seemed extraordinary.

Just about then, the chef came into the living room and set a small tray of coffee things on the table beside him.

"Thanks," Disun said, pouring himself a mug, then taking a quick sip while focusing once again on the TV. The news was winding to an end and the presenter was once again running through the news highlights. Then something caught Disun's attention. He sat forward on the sofa.

The photograph that suddenly came up on the TV screen was unmistakeable. Disun froze, coffee mug mid-way to his open lips. What in the world was happening!

.... And to wrap up the news highlights for this morning, we regret to announce, once again, that popular Lagos Socialite and Businessman, Mr Ige Gabriele Olukayode is in critical condition at a Lagos Hospital after suffering multiple gunshot wounds from unknown assailants in the wee hours of this morning. There are preliminary indications that Mr Olukayode was returning from a late night visit to his close friend and associate – Mr Disun Falodun – who also recently lost his father in the aftermath of a botched kidnapping. While some believe that this was a robbery attack, others speculate that the attack could have been the repercussion of a corporate feud. Rumours also abound of possible reprisal from a Chicago-based cartel with which Mr Olukayode had supposedly had previous dealings. There are no concrete facts at the moment as the police are still carrying on their investigations. Mr Olukayode however remains unconscious as doctors continue to battle for his life. While wishing him full recovery, our thoughts and prayers are with his loved ones.

Disun's jaw dropped and the coffee mug fell from his hand, tumbling over his lap and exploding with a loud shatter as it landed on the marble floor. He seemed to have suddenly lost all senses of control and coordination. Suddenly, every telephone in the house came alive at the same time, enveloping the building in a strange, harrowing whine.

ACKNOWLEDGEMENTS

Special thanks to The All-Knowing for unremitting Guidance and Grace; to my parents for sowing invaluable seeds; to my family for showing remarkable poise, facing rivalry from my art and commerce; to my earliest punters for their thoughts and foresight; to the editors for applying their best intuitions; to the designers, developers, photographers, artists and reviewers for their creative and constructive say; and, to all my readers for taking the ride. I earnestly thank you all.

GLOSSARY

419	Criminal code for financial fraud and similar crimes
A o t'olohun	We are not comparable to God
A ta koro wo'nu ado, ko le mu omo inu e woo	He who magically disappears into a gourd could not take his descendants with him
A ti dupe	We have given thanks
Aadun	Traditional snack made with corn flour and palm oil
Abeg	*Pidgin:* I beg; Please
Abeg, make I go see for myself	*Pidgin:* Please allow me to (go and) see this for myself
Abela Meje	(Religious candles involving the use of) Seven Candles
Abi?	*Interjection:* Right? Isn't it? Etc
Afopino	Moth
Agbada	Traditional three-piece garment, including a flowing robe - similar to a *Babariga*
Agbedo	*Literally:* We mustn't (say, see, witness, etc); Taboo
Agbo	Traditional medicine, typically based on steamed or fermented leaves, barks and roots
Agunmaniye	*Literally:* Tall without intellect; Also name of fast-growing tree
Akanni	One of many "innate names". Within the Yoruba culture, children are often given these special names capturing their innate essence, or projected personality
Akara	Fried bean cake
Alaafia ...E maa ya'se o	(We are) in good health ...do not relent at work
Alayonbere	A specie of serpentine lizard
Ankara	Coloful cotton textile
Aremo	First-born son
Asee kokoro ti o un j'efo, ara efo lo wa.	*Proverb:* The insect that ravages the lettuce, dwells on the lettuce
Asiri a bo	May (your or our) dignity be preserved
Awelorun	*Literally:* One with wreathed neck; describes physical feature of a woman's whereby her neck appears to be wreathed in soft, supple skin, resulting in rows of horizontal rings etched in the creases of her skin; typically considered a thing of beauty
Awon eleyi	These ones
Awuf dey run belle	*Pidgin; Literally:* Free food runs the bowel. Could mean: "Penny wise, pound foolish."
Ayan	Descendant(s) of a lineage of drummers; a professional drummer
Azan	Islamic call to prayer
Baale	Leader of a small community; lower in status to a monarch
Baba mi	My Father
Babalawo	Native Doctor
Babariga(s)	Traditional three-piece garment(s), including a flowing robe - similar to agbada
Baranda	Con; Swindle; Dupe
Boju-boju	Hide-and-seek

Bournvita	Brand of hot chocolate
Broda	Brother
Broken	Broken English; Pidgin English
Buka	Make-shift canteen
Carnation; Peak; Coast	Brands of canned evaporated milk
Cashie	Gambling game similar to poker
Danfo	*Slang:* Mini-bus (used in City transportation)
Dogonyaro	Tree renown for medicinal qualities; known to cure malaria
E gudu mor'ing o	Good Morning
E kaaro	Good Morning
E pele o	Sorry
E.F.C.C.	Economic and Financial Crime Commission
Eba	Staple meal based on fermented cassava starch
Edika Ikong	Vegetable meal with an assortment of condiments
Eeewo!	Taboo! Abomination!
Eefin ni'wa	*Idiom:* Character is like smoke (it cannot be contained)
Efo-riro	Vegetable meal with an assortment of condiments
Egbirin ote; B'aa se n ge'kan ni'ikan n ruwe	*Idiom:* Conspiratorial faunas; as we prune one, another sprouts
Egin	*Title:* Similar to "Mr" in the dialect of the Ondo people of Western Nigeria
Egusi	(Soup made of ground) Melon seeds
Eko Akete	Lagos; a fond, almost adulatory way of referring to the City
Eko Akete, Ilu Ogbon	Lagos; Land of Enlightening
Eku-eda	Type of rodent
Ekute'le	*Literally:* house-rat; describes same
Eleda	*Literally:* Creator. Also used to describe an individual's spiritual essence, linked to the individual's luck and destiny. Similar to *Ori* and the Ibo *Chi*
Eleenia	A spiritual being. Also one of the nick-names of legendary Afro Beat musician - Fela Anikulapo-Kuti
Emere	Spirit Child
Epa	Type of masquerade
Epa n pa ara e, o l'ohun n p'aja	*Proverb:* The tick is killing itself, while believing it is killing the dog
Esu laalu, ogiri oko	*Literally: Esu laalu*, (recipient) wall of projectile stones. Name and sobriquet of an ancient Yoruba deity, often equated to the devil
Face-me-I-face-you	*Slang:* (Building containing) one-room apartments arranged in two parallel rows facing each other, separated by a corridor
Feragamo	Italian (fashion) designer; products thereof
Fever, koo, fever niiii	*Literally:* It isn't and it is fever; typically used in sarcarsm
Fitila	Earthen oil lamp
Fuji	Popular genre of indegenous music
Garri	Nigerian Staple made of fermented, dried cassava (becomes *Eba* when cooked)
Gbe enu e soun. Koye wo ni brother e?	*Derog; Literally:* (Put your mouth away…) Shut up; which Koye is your brother?
Gbe'na g'ori ota	*Slang: Literally:* Light fire upon the head of your enemy.
Gbegiri	Soup made with ground beans

Gbetu-gbetu	Feared goat-horn charm famed for its efficacy at rendering its victims invalid
Haba	*Interjection:* An exclamation of disbelief, disapproval, resentment, etc; similar to "Come on"
He dey follow us?	*Pidgin:* Is he following us?
Idi-Ileke	*Literally:* "Hip-of-beads"; pet name, usually for a highly contoured woman, emanating, perhaps, from the fact that women of such endowment would often wear ornate beads around their waist, especially in the olden days
Ifa	Yoruba Oracle; also refers to the underlining religion and unwritten verses (*Odu Ifa*) upon which the knowledge and practice is based
Ifoti-olooyi	A slap to the face (distinguished by the spinning action it typically induces in its recipient)
Igbira	Nigerian tribe
Ige adubi!	Special "innate" name for a child born feet first. *Adubi* literally means "one born with exertion"
Ika o dogba	*Idiom; Literally:* Fingers are not equal; metaphor for the (social) inequality amongst people
Ikongusi	Therapeutic stream in Ondo State
Ikoto	Traditional spinning top or spin top toy, often made of snail shells or improvised random items
Ikun	Ground Squirrel
Ina-ore	*Literally:* "Flame of Friendship". Tiny, shinny, tattoo-like spot left on the back of the hand after a smouldering, charcoaly matchstick had been stuck to the skin in a moonlight game of friendship and valour played by young children
Isale oro, o l'egbin	The bottom of wealth is filthy
Iwo	You
Iwo ko l'o da mi ... Iwo ko l'o dami; O si n wuwa bi Eledumare ... Iwo ko lo dam iii!	Ancient rhyme: You aren't my creator; yet you are behaving like The *Eledumare* (Yoruba for God)!
Iya-Ilu	*Literally:* Mother of Drums: Type of drum, hung on the shoulder, beaten with a curved stick and coaxed to "verbalise" rhythmic, discernable statements; also called the "talking drum"
Iyalode	Highest chieftaincy title attainable by a woman within the king's cabinet. (There are many prominent Iyalodes in Yoruba history)
Jagbajantus	*Slang:* Nonsense
Jobele	Leaf of a tropical plant
K'ama ri	*Interjection:* Shall we not witness it. Taboo.
Ke	*Interjection:* Similar to "really" used for emphasis or in cynicism
Kia-kia	Right now; right away
Lagbo-lagbo	Large, colourful banquets often held on a shut-down street and often with a full band in attendance
Lahilah, illahlah	*Arabic:* Allah (God) is the Greatest
Ma ko ba mi	Do not compromise me; do not bring problems to me
Mallam	*Hausa:* "Mr"
Me Chai	*Hausa:* Tea Merchant

Mentholatum	Brand of Mentholated Ointment
Mo da'ran	I am in trouble
Moin-moin	Steamed beans pudding
Molue	Improvised buses fabricated on lorry chassis. Primary mode of mass transportation in Lagos up till the early 2000s
Mullah	(Formerly) a Muslim scholar, teacher, or religious leader: recently used as a title of respect. *Slang:* someone of worth
O	*Interjection:* Used at the end of a statement for emphasis
O ti loyun, abi?	You are pregnant, aren't you?
O tu'n bere?	You are still inquiring?
Obalende	Section of Lagos Island
Obirin ajodi	Foreign or alien woman
Odu	*Slang:* Illicit activity
Oga	Boss
Ogbeni	Yoruba for "Mr"
Ogbologbo	(Criminal) Kingpin. *Slang:* Criminally-cool, especially when used playfully among friends
Ogi	Corn pap
Okada	*Slang:* (City transportation system based on the) motorcycle; derived from the name of a pioneering indigenous airliner being that the motorcycles essentially "fly"
Okete	Large rodent
Oko	A projectile stone
Oko mi	My husband
Okunrin Mejo	*Literally:* Eight Men; typically used in salutation to a man of stregth and/or character
Ole	Thief
Ologbojo	Type of rodent
Olohun o ni je	God forbid
Oloriburuku	*Literally:* the Bad-headed one; derogatory
Oluwole	Lagos Island market renown for its many trades
Omele	Type of drum
Omolanke	Improvised wooden cart used in the City to transport goods
Ori e o da	*Literally:* Your head is bad; meaning: you're crazy
Ori-olori	*Literally:* Someone else's head: *Slang:* Fake Passport
Oro o ki n tobi ki a fi obe laa	*Idiom:* A disclosure is never daunting enough to warrant reduction by a knife
Ote	Conspiracy; cold war
Owu-ikorun	Thin black thread used for decorating women's hair in a techniques loosely similar to plaiting
Oya	Type of large rodent
Oya (2)	Shall we? Right away; let's go, etc
Oya n'le	Let's go home
Pa enu e mo! O ti yee... o ti ye eleyi na	Shut your mouth. You have survived this predicament; you have survived in any case
Paraga	Cocktail blend including alcohol, medicine and a wide range of (narcotic) condiments
Pele, oko mi	Sorry, my husband

Pepsodent	Brand of toothpaste
Piri lolongo n'ji; a o kin gbo ku eye lori ite; piri lologo n ji...	*Incantation:* One never finds a dead bird in its net, etc… (Yoruba incantations are often composed of know natural facts mixed with coded historical facts and hidden mystical knowledge.)
Pregnancy ke? Ma'a mi Pregnancy Bawo?	Pregnancy, really? Mother, pregnancy in what sense?
Pscphew!	*Interjection:* An expression of disdain, disapproval or perplexity referred to as an "*ose*"
Puff-puff	Fried Buns
Pure water	Ubiquitous commercial drinking water sold in plastic sachets
Rikisi, Arekereke, tembelekun	Various manifestations of intrigue; shenanigans
Sabo	Small settlement of people of one ethnicity within the geographic community of another. In Western Nigeria, this term typically describes settlement of the *Hausa* people
Sango	Ancient deity of Thunder
Sekere	Musical instrument composing of a large gourd covered with a cowry-bearing mesh. (Cowry was the ancient currency of the Yorubas)
Shawa	Type of dried fish
Shepe, opa-eyin	Cocktail blend including alcohol, medicine and a wide range of (narcotic) condiments. (Similar to *paraga*)
Sokoto-1	Trousers
Sokoto-2	Northern Nigerian City; also name of the State
St. Louis	Brand of Sugar
St. Morris	Brand of cigarette
Sutana	White religious robe as adopted by some Christian sects
Suwe	Competitive game typically played by young girls
Suya	Popular spiced-meat barbecue of Northern-Nigerian origin
Taba-taba, kuli-kuli, chuku-chuku, panbola-bola, chin-chin	Various kinds of sweet treats
Tesbiu	Islamic praying beads
Ti a ba ni omi lo maa se eja jina	*Proverb:* Who would have imagined that it is water in which a fish thrives that would cook it to perfection
Ti a ba ran'ni ni'se eru, aa fi t'omo je	*Proverb:* When assigned with the duty of a slave, one delivers as a blue-blood"
Tiroo	Traditional eye-liner
Tuwo-shinkafi	Hausa staple made with mashed rice
Wallahi	*Arabic:* Allah (God) is my Witness
Wetin Dey Happen	*Pidgin:* What is happening?
Wetin you want? You no go fit come here dey harass …	*Pidgin:* What do you want? You cant come here to harass…
Yeeeeparirpa	*Interjection:* An exclamation of sudden fear, concern, disbelief, etc
Yeepa … ori mi o …	*Interjection: Yeepa:* Short form of yeeparipa; *Ori mi o:* Literally: My head; however references the spiritual head. Within the Yoruba culture, this "head" is believed to control luck, destiny, karma, etc; similar to *Eleda* and the Ibo *Chi*
Yiyo ekun … bi ti t'ojo ko kee	*Proverb:* The tiger's stealth must not be mistaken for cowardice

BARON OF BROAD STREET

CPSIA information can be obtained at www.ICGtesting.com
Printed in the USA
LVOW11s1300271015

459795LV00042B/617/P

9 781329 427532